THE ORESTEIA

Aeschylus' greatest work unfolds the history of a family destroying itself under a blood curse.

In The Agamemnon, *the first play of the trilogy, the vengeful Clytemnestra murders her hero-husband Agamemnon for his sacrifice of their daughter Iphigenia.* The Libation Bearers *concerns Orestes, the son of Agamemnon and Clytemnestra. Encouraged by his sister Electra, he plots his mother's death to avenge his father's murder.*

In The Eumenides *Orestes is hounded by the Furies; a victim of his own guilt, he is driven from shore to shore for his crime of matricide. The forceful power of Aeschylus reaches full climax in this third play. Orestes epitomizes the timeless tragedy and triumph of man—the hero who struggles to a divine destiny through his own free and indomitable will.*

Paul Roche's dramatic re-creations into English poetry of The Orestes Plays of Aeschylus *are (in his own words) "the closest to the originals in sound, sense, and feeling that I could contrive." Included in this Mentor edition are a glossary of classical names and places and an informal survey of the Greek theater.*

Literature of Ancient Greece
in MENTOR Books

THE
ORESTES PLAYS
of
Aeschylus

THE AGAMEMNON
THE LIBATION BEARERS
THE EUMENIDES

A NEW TRANSLATION BY
Paul Roche

A MENTOR BOOK from
NEW AMERICAN LIBRARY
TIMES MIRROR
New York and Scarborough, Ontario
The New English Library Limited, London

Library of Congress Catalog Card No. 63-9436

 MENTOR TRADEMARK REG. U.S. PAT. OFF. AND FOREIGN COUNTRIES
REGISTERED TRADEMARK—MARCA REGISTRADA
HECHO EN CHICAGO, U.S.A.

SIGNET, SIGNET CLASSICS, MENTOR, PLUME AND MERIDIAN BOOKS
are published *in the United States* by
The New American Library, Inc.,
1301 Avenue of the Americas, New York, New York 10019,
in Canada by The New American Library of Canada Limited,
81 Mack Avenue, Scarborough, Ontario MIL 1M8,
in the United Kingdom by The New English Library Limited,
Barnard's Inn, Holborn, London, E.C. 1, England.

8 9 10 11 12 13 14 15 16

PRINTED IN THE UNITED STATES OF AMERICA

ΤΟΥΑΙΣΧΥΛΟΥΑΓΑΜΕΜΝΩΝ

ΘΕΟΥΣΜΕΝΑΙΤΩΤΩΝΔΑΠΑΛΛΑΓΗΠΟΝΩΝ
ΦΡΟΥΡΑΣΕΤΕΙΑΣΜΗΚΟΣΗΝΚΟΙΜΩΜΕΝΟΣ
ΣΤΕΓΑΙΣΑΤΡΕΙΔΩΝΑΓΚΑΘΕΝΚΥΝΟΣΔΙΚΗΝ
ΑΣΤΡΩΝΚΑΤΟΙΔΑΝΥΚΤΕΡΩΝΟΜΗΓΥΡΙΝ
ΚΑΙΤΟΥΣΦΕΡΟΝΤΑΣΧΕΙΜΑΚΑΙΘΕΡΟΣΒΡΟΤΟΙΣ
ΛΑΜΠΡΟΥΣΔΥΝΑΣΤΑΣΕΜΠΡΕΠΟΝΤΑΣΑΙΘΕΡΙ

THE ORESTEIA

The *Oresteia* is the story of a self-assertive, self-sufficient house in division against itself, cursed onward through three stages of self-propelled disaster (murder, matricide, and madness) to the last point of disintegration . . . finally broken, and thus saved, in the person of Orestes, who, divinely chastened and accepting a viable pattern of relationships among honor, justice, and personal fulfillment, inaugurates a new era of creatural cooperation and harmony.

CONTENTS

THE
ORESTES PLAYS
of
Aeschylus

INTRODUCTION

I THE MESSAGE OF AESCHYLUS

In spite of the distance in time and of a theatrical convention strange to us, what Greek tragedy, and especially the *Oresteia* of Aeschylus, has to say to the inner ears of our consciousness is no less germane to our society than it was to the simpler and less perplexed men and women of his own generation. *Our* temptations to pride are subtler. We, with our abundant awareness and miraculous discoveries, fall more easily into the complicated arrogance of believing that we make our own knowledge and know only what we can prove— thereby severing ourselves in one confused stroke from the wealth of all that is. We are at once too clever and too simple, putting immense faith in our statistics and our abstruse planning, and forgetting that systems can rinse away three quarters of reality. There are many things we need to be reminded of: that fullness of knowledge reveals itself not so much to the dispassionate intellect as to the whole sentient self; that it is not a worship of uniformity and static patterns that makes a man, but individuality and difference; that the prize of an integral personality is not won through trying to be normal but by a passionate grasping of life at the heights, where

the very danger of our aspirations should become the
bedrock of our humility. These may not be the most obvious lessons to take away from Greek tragedy, but they
are there, as well as others more fundamental. At the
bottom of everything lies the conviction that we are be-
holden to some higher purpose and power, some in-
escapable principle outside ourselves. It is part of that
indefatigable Necessity behind all our lives—a terror and
ultimately a death—which we must face, not merely at
the end but all the way through, if the salt of our
existence is not to lose its savor.

We tend, of course, to think that someone who lived
two thousand four hundred years ago could not possibly
have anything to say to us: the hypersensitive, sophisticated progeny of an atomic age. We are wrong. Circumstances may change but the human being does not.
Pride is still pride, fear fear, hate hate. Only the setting changes. What Aeschylus proclaims through his
three great plays—*The Agamemnon, The Libation Bearers,* and *The Eumenides*—is a manifesto on Man perpetually valid.

The *Oresteia* is the story of an aristocratic house in
the process of destroying itself under a hereditary curse,
which is both a destiny and a free expression of love and
hate. The blood feud can end only by total self-destruc-
tion, or by giving way to a divinely established justice
which is itself evolving—evolving from primitive con-
cepts of retribution into a higher order of compassion,
enlightenment, and peace. Artistically, it is the master
work of the acknowledged master of lyric tragedy. It is
our only extant trilogy, since the three plays of
Sophocles in the Oedipus cycle are not strictly a trilogy.
Aside from it only four plays by Aeschylus have survived out of a possible ninety.

The unfailing youthfulness of the Greek myths as handled by the three great dramatists lies in their appeal
alike to the intelligence, the emotions, and the imagination. They appeal to the intelligence because some
solid consideration underlies the dramatic events, some

positive assertion concretely presented about existence which invites conclusions to be drawn from it. Their events are so striking and so unusual that they arouse the curiosity to ask what they mean.[1]

What the *Oresteia* means, of course, is enshrined in its story, its μῦθος or myth, which Aeschylus took from an age some six or seven hundred years before his own. He uses this as a vehicle, a symbol, of preoccupations that go far beyond the murder of a king with its train of retributions, go beyond even the political and moral interests of Aeschylus's own fifth-century Athens—though to these they give a distance, dignity, and clarity which double the purgative and sublimatory power of tragedy.

Each play is complete, and each has its own formative, imaginative plan, but the whole is more than the parts, and the three plays provide in mythical form, inspired by unfailing magnificence of poetry, a theme of first importance for Athens, the role of the state as champion of justice.[2]

Behind the domestic tragedy of Agamemnon and Clytemnestra, behind the disturbing problems of Athenian democracy, there are higher strata of significance which transcend, even while they deepen and tauten, the plot and problems of each individual play. We are made to see the universal plot of life against death, honor against degradation, beauty and goodness against ugliness and evil: eternal issues presented to us in such a way that for once we can go beyond those final abstractions which outstrip our emotional responses and see how divine laws operate through human life, and, seeing, understand what it is to be a man. For man's relation to the divine is not abstract but concrete. The human is patterned on the divine even if we can understand the divine only by battening on the human. The glories of

[1] C. M. Bowra, *The Greek Experience.* New York: The World Publishing Company, 1957; The New American Library (Mentor Books), 1959.
[2] *Ibid.*

Greek sculpture—Olympia, Delphi, the Parthenon—show how the beauty of man bursts into strength and joy when the gods inspire him. So Aeschylus shows us that the behavior of men is fraught with a significance that is tremendous because it is related to the divine. We are borne upward through ascending levels of import till the original characters, the particular and the personal, in the very process of working out their destinies, stand for a conflict of forces which play upon one another, leaven one another, evolve and mount to the throne of Zeus himself; and Zeus too is evolving.

It goes without saying that Aeschylus was a pioneer in many of his most telling thoughts, delving and making distinctions which were at once simple and complete. I believe that pitted against some of the cleverest of us he would be found a pioneer still. What modern legislator dares to give so downright an assent to the fundamental concept of good government—maximum *liberty* consonant with order—as Aeschylus does in *The Eumenides* when he has Athena wish for something between authority and anarchy for her people? And how many psychologists and psychiatrists of the last seventy years have been so refreshingly realistic as to say: "Don't try to do away with fear altogether. Keep it in its right proportions: for what human being was ever good who had no fear?"

It is precisely this touch, this ability to realize that nobody can even cross the road alive without such a thing as fear, that differentiates the lover from the betrayer of reality. We see it again in Aeschylus's handling of justice. He makes distinctions which sheer brain could so easily have missed. What sociologist could imbue us with a more thorough sense of the hopeless injustice of self-exacted justice, and yet of our commitment to some kind of redressing of the balance, than Aeschylus does in *The Libation Bearers* when, even while he is showing us the corrosive action of private hate and the cruelty, stupidity, and suffering of war, he devotes a whole play to the notion that we cannot simply stand aside and watch a murder? Out-and-out pacifism is as wrong as out-and-out war. After all we *are* our brother's—here, our father's—keeper.

Aeschylus pushes through to the most baffling distinctions of all: personal responsibility, fate, freedom, sin, justice, the dominion of Providence. No false simplifications are allowed, and no glib philosophy. In each of these plays we are made to see truths which we should never have forgotten. At the cost of leaving things barely etched against their primal mystery, Aeschylus shows us that we *are* after all responsible for what we do, even though we may not be responsible for the circumstances that make us do them. Orestes *was* to blame for murdering his mother even if it was a god who urged him to it. Clytemnestra *did* commit a crime when she killed her husband, even though everything about him cried for the chastisement of pride and slaughter. All human action is a dilemma between good and evil; or, more metaphysically, between good and good. *That* is our glory—to be willing to accept the pain and the risk of commitment, when it would be safer and more comfortable to pretend that we cannot do right and cannot do wrong; that no god cares; and that no eternal contradictions are written in our hearts.

The theme of all tragedy is the sadness of life and the universality of evil. The inference the Greeks drew from this was *not* that life was not worth living, but that because it was worth living the obstacles to it were worth overcoming. Tragedy is the story of our existence trying to rear its head above the general shambles. The worst and final temptation, no less for us than for an Athenian of the fifth century B.C., is to stop the fight and slide into inactivity of heart and will. The final paradox is that in every acceptance of the challenge we encounter both our glory and our victimhood. The fatal mistake of an Oedipus is not that he murders his father and marries his mother, but that his own integrity is coupled with overweening self-confidence and through it he finds himself out. The tragedy of a Clytemnestra is not that she does away with her husband, but that she can no longer respect him and refuses to take the easy way out by letting him live. The tragedy, the dilemma, of an Orestes is not that he murders his mother, but that he is horribly aware of the enormity of matricide and faces it as a duty.

It is precisely through the courage of each of these characters to choose his fate and abide by his divine victimhood that he reaches through to greatness—even though with Clytemnestra destiny comes with the stroke that fells her. Behind everything, like a luminous measurement to human values, and as the criterion of all ethical sanctions, is the felt presence of a celestial order. In the highest and finest reaches of Greek culture—as in the unreasoned conviction of our own instinct—the beauty of the human lies in its proximity to the divine. "We must as far as possible make ourselves immortal," as Aristotle says, and thereby worship incorruptible beauty and unfailing strength. Paradoxically, we are what we are because God is what he is, and not vice versa.

II   THE FORMAL IMPACT OF AESCHYLUS

Aeschylus was born at Eleusis in Attica in 525 B.C., though the date is by no means certain. He was destined to live well on into the heart of Greece's golden age: the age which saw Athens rise to the pinnacle of her greatness. But Aeschylus was never forced to witness, as did Sophocles, his great successor and rival, all this glory crumble into the disaster of the Peloponnesian War, with poverty-stricken but victorious Sparta standing over the ruins of Athens.

Although Aeschylus wrote at least one drama which dealt with contemporary history—*The Persians*—the three plays by which he is most remembered, the trilogy of the *Oresteia,* plunge into events which took place many hundreds of years before. Aeschylus was several centuries too late to set sail with Agamemnon and the Greek armada to recover Helen and punish Troy. Yet he might have done so, for he too was a hero and as a young man had lived in a heroic age. He fought with the Athenian ten thousand brave who upset the army launched against Greece from Persia, on the plains of Marathon. It is probable that ten years later he fought again in the critical sea battle off the island of Salamis, in which the Greeks under Themistocles destroyed the Persian fleet and thus cut off from supplies the fabulous army of Xerxes. These were two of the great events in Aeschylus's life, and when he came to die in faraway Sicily at the court of King Hieron, his lifelong patron —old and successful and not unloved—he seems to have been thinking not about his ninety plays or the prize he won thirteen times, but that as a young man he had played his part as a soldier in saving Greece. The famous epitaph which he composed for himself is redolent with pride:

> Aeschylus, Euphorion's son, this tablet hides
> Who passed away in Gela where the wheatfields grow:
> His bravery the glorious shrine of Marathon can tell
> Where the deep-maned Medes had learnt it well.

The year of his death is usually given as 456 B.C. The Geloans honored him with a state funeral, and he was mourned in Athens.

The stamp of Aeschylus's soul was loyal, heroic, aristocratic, and uncompromising. It was also vigorous, ingenious, and profound. There was a great deal of the inspired prophet about him—the seer, lofty and penetrating in thought, delving into the past and casting his look far into the future. What he saw he sent flooding out of him, crashing down in thunderous poetry. There was a kind of divine impetus in him that struck out great rending thoughts in magnificent language and could never let him wait for the absolute refinement, for the perfect balance of a deliberate and conscious art. Aeschylus did not have the patience to charm and restrain, like Sophocles, whose poetry seeps into the heart by an artistry consummately, but illusively, natural, or tolerant like Euripides, with an inner pathos for the weaknesses and fears of the human psyche. His vision of heaven and earth was both grand and overwhelming. Aeschylus never minded if he shocked, "startling men by strange *tours de force;* coming into direct collision with their feelings, moral, political and religious": [3] people must be made to see the truth even if it shook them.

His personal temperament seems to have matched his genius:

> vehement, passionate, irascible; writing his tragedies (as later critics judged) as if half-drunk, doing (as Sophocles said of him) what was right in his art without knowing why; following the impulses that led him to strange themes and dark problems, rather than aiming at the perfection of a complete, all-sided culture; frowning with shaggy brows, like a wild bull, glaring fiercely, and bursting into a storm of wrath when annoyed by critics or rival poets; a Marlowe rather than a Shakespeare.[4]

His style of writing is all these things: majestic, flaming, close-packed, loaded; "pegged and wedged and dovetailed," as Aristophanes called it; teeming with strange compound epithets which are nevertheless amazingly well-fitted to the facts, and drawn from a range of experience which shies at nothing—whether it be the nature of Zeus himself or the absurdity of war. It is the grand style par excellence; and the essence of the grand

---

[3] E. H. Plumtre, in his *Tragedies of Aeschylus,* New York: David McKay, Inc., drawing his portrait from almost the only extant sources: the Medicean Ms., Plutarch, Aristophanes (*The Frogs*), Athenaeus, and a few scattered allusions in contemporary or all but contemporary authors.
[4] *Ibid.*

style is to exalt human experience above the merely human view of it. His is not a language that can be spoken in the market place, compounded as it is of the lyric and epic riches of the past with the neologisms of the present; but it is a language that can put us in touch with the human on a divine plane and make us see ourselves as we might or ought to be. . . . A glorious if a dangerous conception, for it needs but a tilt to tip the sublime into the ridiculous—a tumble which Aeschylus himself does not always avoid.

It is a conception, too, which perfectly tallies with his own view of the theater as a place where the eyes as well as the ears could be stunned into attention. Whether we can admit all the instances Professor Plumtre gives of this, there is no final proving, but they do indicate a love of spectacle on a new scale: the introduction of freakish animals on the stage, dragons with wings, beasts half cock half horse, or half goat and half stag, dragging the chariot of Oceanus in the *Prometheus,* or flying with Athena through the air with her shield billowing like a sail. He is said to have clothed his actors in costumes so splendid that the priests in the temples copied them for vestments and hierophants used them in their mysteries. He could make a sensation of silence itself: putting a character in the forefront of his drama and never having him say a word. In *The Eumenides* (the last play we have of his, written at the age of sixty-seven, some three years before his death) he brought onto the stage a chorus of terrifying ugliness, the Erinyes or Furies: misshapen crones snorting and wailing, blackskinned and draped in black, scarlet tongues lolling from the masks of their mouths. If they were fifty in number —as is possible—perhaps it is true that children went into fits and women had miscarriages. Nor can we wonder that he fell into one of his recurrent periods of disfavor, with the old charges leveled against him: that he was trying to dishonor holy things.

Be that as it may, when we put on his plays we can be fairly certain that Aeschylus was a master of style not only in words but in spectacle as well: song and stately dance, costumes, scenery, processionals, and decorations. He designed his dramas as visions as much as poems. We should realize too that he was a master of dramatic time—its inventor to all intents and purposes —exploiting a sense of duration that was Bergsonian. He transposed past, present, and future into quickly sliding states of memory and consciousness, thus anticipating Joyce and Virginia Woolf by two thousand four hundred years. He could work on several temporal levels at once, as if time were not so much a sequence of events— "numerus motus secundum prius et posterius," as Aristotle's definition was going to be—as an unavoidable circumference of activity, whereon any point of the past is simultaneous with the present, and the future already impinges, folded within the vast interior arc of reality. Not until Shakespeare did any poet send out his tendrils in so many directions at once; and not until the art of the cinema did techniques of running the past and the elsewhere into the present and here—with cutbacks, dissolving scenes, memories, and monologues breaking into pictures—receive the final treatment that was inevitable.

Hythe, Kent
September 25, 1962

THE PEDIGREE OF SIN

(past and to come)

(i)   Tantalus killed his son and served him up to the gods as food; (they restored him to life and punished Tantalus).

(ii) Atreus killed Thyestes' young children and served them up to him at a banquet of "reconciliation."

(iii) Helen deserted her husband and went to Troy with Paris.

(iv) Agamemnon sacrificed at the altar his daughter Iphigenia.

(v)   Aegisthus becomes the lover of Clytemnestra.

(vi) Agamemnon brazenly brings Cassandra back with him from Troy.

(vii) Clytemnestra (with Aegisthus) kills Agamemnon.

(viii) Orestes kills Clytemnestra and Aegisthus.

THE PLOTS

The Agamemnon: Agamemnon returns from the Trojan War victorious but doomed.

The Libation Bearers: Orestes comes back from exile to avenge his father's death. With the help of his sister, Electra, he plots his mother's death.

The Eumenides: Orestes, hounded by the Furies for the crime of matricide, flees to Athena for forgiveness. Athena establishes a new court of justice; frees Orestes from his guilt; placates the Furies by making them protectoresses of Athens and changing their names to the "Eumenides" or "Merciful Ones."

THE

AGAMEMNON

for ANNE FREMANTLE

Virisque adquirit eundo

Virgil

(She gathers strength at every step)

THE CHARACTERS

AGAMEMNON: King of Argos, and son of ATREUS

CLYTEMNESTRA: his wife

CASSANDRA: captured daughter of King PRIAM

AEGISTHUS: lover of CLYTEMNESTRA

WATCHMAN: of the King's palace

HERALD: from AGAMEMNON's army

CHORUS: of Argive elders

Attendants of CLYTEMNESTRA
Retinue of AGAMEMNON
Bodyguard of AEGISTHUS

TIME AND SETTING

It is the heroic age: several hundred years before the time of Aeschylus or Pericles. The siege of Troy has been in progress for a decade and from the start CLYTEMNESTRA has never ceased to brood over AGAMEMNON'S sacrifice of their daughter IPHIGENIA (made to supplicate favorable winds for the Greek armada). She has taken as lover AEGISTHUS, her husband's enemy and cousin—who has his own score to settle with the king. For it was AEGISTHUS's father, THYESTES, to whom AGAMEMNON'S father, ATREUS, served up his own children to eat at a banquet. The fact that this was done as a reprisal for THYESTES's having seduced his brother's wife made no difference. AEGISTHUS now feels it incumbent on him to avenge his father and so add the next link in the chain of family crime. The queen too has been waiting. She has posted a WATCHMAN on the roof of the royal palace at Argos to tell her the exact moment when the beacons will flash home the news of Troy's downfall, and so the end of the war and the imminent return of her husband.

THE

AGAMEMNON

WATCHMAN

O you gods! how I long for an end to all this strain:
This year-long watch, up on the roof of the Atreidae,
Crouched on my elbows like a kennel hound,
Scanning by heart the stars at night,
That chorus of the master shiners,
Dispensers of our summers and our storms—
Those so conspicuous stars: their wax and wane—
For I am watching still for one bright sign:
A beacon flash from Troy to tell me it is taken.
Yes, it's fixed on that, this woman's man-strong heart,
With all a female's longing.

There's my bed: dew-drenched, tossed, untouched by
                                                dreams;
Fear, not sleep, my comrade;
Eyelids trussed from ever sleeping safely.
And if I whistle, then, hum a little ditty,
Just a tune to charm and drug sleep off,
Oh, it turns into a dirge for this stricken house—
So gone down, so fallen from its governance.
How I wish there'd come at last a happy end to strain!

Oh make that bonfire blaze
Good news upon the gloom.

> [*A beacon flare slowly
> spreads across the dawn*]

A light! Oh look:
Lovely dayspring in the dark,
Forerunner of that chorus and the dance
Which many in Argos shall celebrate this day.

Hullo, there! Hullo!
Cry out the news to Agamemnon's queen.
Let the lady rise with instant shout and sing
Her welcome to the beacon . . .
If that clarion flash be true
And Troy great city fallen.
I'll start a dance myself; the dice are tumbling well.
My master's lucky throw is mine:
That bonfire's scored a triple-six.
Master, may you soon come home and I
Grasp in this hand the hand I love.

The rest I leave to silence—
A giant ox treads on my tongue.
Though if these walls could find a voice,
They'd say it plain.
As for me: I'll let the knowing know,
But with those others—let my memory go.

[*The* WATCHMAN *disappears from the roof. Meanwhile
the glad voice of* CLYTEMNESTRA *can be heard from
within. At her bidding, attendants carrying torches and
incense go round kindling fires at the altars. The*
CHORUS *of old men enters chanting*]

PARODOS

Now is the tenth year since Priam's
Double and deadly match, the Atreidae,
King Menelaus and King Agamemnon,
By grace of God doubly princes—
Each with a scepter, each with a throne—

Dispatched their armada in succor from Argos:
A thousand shouting ships of line,
Screaming like eagles high and disconsolate
Which circle and beat with the blade of their wings
Over ruin of their eyrie, wreck of their young.
But a god—was it Pan, Apollo, or Zeus?—
Hearing from heaven the cry and the pang
Of the dispossessed birds [1] (those guests in his realm),
Sends in the fullness of time the Avenger.

[*The doors of the palace open to disclose* CLYTEMNESTRA
*offering up incense and oil at the altar. The dawn has
now broken*]

So did great Zeus, guardian of etiquette,
Send Atreus' sons hot against Paris,
Starting for Greeks and for Trojans the struggle:
Javelins a-splinter, knees in the dust,
All for the sake of a many-manned woman.
So it stands as it stands, unfolds to its fate.
No balm and no tears, no fire can burn
The gods' wrath away from a sacrifice spurned.

[CLYTEMNESTRA, *with oil and incense in her hands and
surrounded by torchbearers, appears at the top of the
palace steps. She motions the procession to halt as she
stands there listening*]

We're the deserted ones, senile carcasses,
Left behind by those glorious armies,
Leaning our baby-weight fraily on crutches.
Youth's surge in our hearts is futile with age.
Mars is misplaced; our greenery gone.
Dotage advances, totters along
Its three-footed way no more than a child:
Weak as a noonday dream.

[*The old men turn toward* CLYTEMNESTRA *as she proceeds silently down the steps on her way to the various
altars*]

1 Symbolizing the Greeks as led by Agamemnon and Menelaus.

But you, Clytemnestra, Queen,
Tyndareus' daughter,
What's afoot? What news? What message has hastened
you
To go in procession round blazing oblations?
The altars of all our city's protectors—
The gods up above and gods down below,
Gods of the heavens and gods of the market place—
Are flaming with sacrifice.
A hundred fires go staggering upward
High as the sky in a hundred places:
Fueled so purely, balmed so persuasively,
With oils from the sacred resources of princes.
What may you say of this? What dare you tell us,
To soothe away our looming perplexity?
One minute fear has us, one minute hope—
Smiling from altars blandly disarming
The terror, the rawness—insatiable sorrow—
Of all our soul's corroding.

[*Without a word,* CLYTEMNESTRA *goes into the palace.
The* CHORUS *regroups and the rhythm changes. The old
men chant in strophe and antistrophe, telling of the
omen which preceded their leaders' departure for Troy,
and of the terrible sacrifice of* IPHIGENIA *by* AGAMEMNON]

Strophe 1—First Stasimon

But those redoubtable heroes
Blessedly speeded with omens—
Their saga at least I can sing.
For even senility still
Can draw on the breath of the gods
To cast a spell with song.

I tell how the might of Achaea,
Two-throned,[2] singlehearted
(Kings of the youth of Hellas),
Was tossed full-tilt against Troy

---

[2] Agamemnon and Menelaus shared the Greek leadership. *See* ATRIDAE
in glossary.

By the portentous birds of prowess:
Monarchs of birds to the monarchs
Of ships of the line they alighted:
Black one—one backed silver;
Standing out emblazoned
On the spear-hand side of the palace;
Plunging beaks in a pregnant
Burgeoning hare with litter—
Snatched from her homeward sally.

Sing of sorrow, sorrow,
But let the good prevail.

Antistrophe 1

Then the perspicacious
Seer of our armies,[3] seeing
Into the different hearts
Of the fighting twin Atreidae,
Knew them for the tearing
Falcons of the hare—
Leaders of the host—
And thus foretold the omen:

"The beleaguerers in time
Shall pounce on Priam's city,
Before whose bastions Fate
Shall scatter and consume
The people's wealth and cattle.
But first take care
No rankling god shall blacken
The mighty muzzle forged
By our battering battalions
For bridling Troy.

"For Artemis [4] the chaste one
Rages in her pity:
Those flying dogs her father's

---

[3] Calchas, the prophet.
[4] Artemis, goddess of the hunt, was also the champion of wild animals. The eagles still stand for Agamemnon and Menelaus. The hare is Iphigenia, whom Agamemnon sacrificed to get good winds for the Greek armada.

Fell on the timorous victim—
Unborn brood and mother.
Yes, Artemis is sickened
At the eagles glutting.

"Sing of sorrow, sorrow,
But let the good prevail.

Epode   *(Plea to* ARTEMIS*)*

"Fair though you be and full of
  Grace to the ravening lions'
  Little fumbling kittens,
  And tender to the suckling young
  Of beasts that rove the wilds—
  Yet may good become the issue
  Of that cruel vision.

(Plea to APOLLO*)*

"Cry, so I cry upon Paean [5]
To keep her from keeping Danaän
Windlocked ships at anchor,
Fastened from their sailing;
Or her forcing another oblation:
Barbarous, not to be feasted, [6]
Breeding suspicion and hatred
In the house where the husband is nothing,
And Wrath is the mistress recoiling,
Crafty, relentless and lurking
To avenge the child she remembers."

So rang the voice
(With blessings besides)
Of Calchas the Prophet:
A dynasty's destiny told
From the wayside birds.
Think of it and sing:

[5] Another name for Apollo (as god of healing): here invoked to pre-
  vent his sister from accomplishing the evil part of the omen.
[6] The sacrifice (still to come) of Iphigenia. There is an echo too of the
  grisly banquet at which Atreus made a dish for Thyestes of his own
  children.

"Sorrow, come sorrow!
But let the good prevail."

Strophe 2

Zeus the unknown god,
If Zeus be his best title—
Hail by that: Incomparable!
Undivinable in style!
Unmatched Zeus—my only hope
Of shedding from my soul
The inept weight of worry.

Antistrophe 2

For he that original giant,
Flushed in his broiling pride,
Ouranos, is forgotten.
The next who came was Cronos:
Thrown three times and gone. Cry out:
"O Zeus you are triumphant!"
And be awarded wise.

Strophe 3

He leads us on the way of wisdom's
Everlasting law that truth
Is only learnt by suffering it.
Ah, in sleep the pain distills,
Bleeding on the memory,
And makes us wise against our wills:
God's grace by solemn force.

Antistrophe 3

So it was that day. The elder
Captain of the Achaean fleet,
Blaming no prophet, bent before
The blasts of fortune. All the Grecian
Sail was held starving against
The port of Chalcis in the racing
Ebb and flow of Aulis sound.

Strophe 4

The winds from Strymon pent them in the port,
  A forced holiday of famine:
      Chaos on board,
Ships and tackle mercilessly flogged,
    Time itself bent double—
The flower of Argos fretted into nothing.
    And finally the seer's voice,
      Lashing against the winds
      And speaking for Artemis,
Proclaimed a palliative more deadly yet [7]. . . .
The sons of Atreus smashed their scepters down
    And could not keep from crying.

Antistrophe 4

Then the elder king found voice and said:
    "This fate is hard to disobey,
      And hard if I obey.
    Sever my child—my palace pearl?
    Bloody my hands in that virgin flood?
A father's hands at the altar side? Oh which
    Is worse? But how can I betray
      My fleet and fail my allies?
    They are right in their fury-bound frenzy
    To imprecate the winds to calm
By the blood of a virgin sacrificed . . .
      I hope it may be well!"

Strophe 5

And once he'd buckled on his need to do it,
His spirit changed, gave vent to wicked airs:
    Was sacrilegious, impious,
    Distorted, contumacious, wild.
So does the heart possessed, pressed on by delusion,

---

[7] The sacrifice of his daughter by Agamemnon. The metaphor of
the hare is inverted: Artemis, who was represented before as being
angry at its being torn by the eagles, is here demanding the destruction of a human being.

Race to its sinning.
Callously, he dealt the deathblow to his daughter:
All for a war waged for a woman—
An offering to the fleet.

Antistrophe 5

Her prayers, her cries of "Father!" and her girlhood
Were nothing to the passion of her jury:
The military minded.
Her father blessed her; told his ministers
To go and take her as she cowered huddled
In her tunic,
And boldly lift her like a goat above the altar;
To gag her lovely mouth and stopper
With cruelty her curses.

Strophe 6

And slipping to the ground her saffròn dress,
She glanced with piteous eyes to wound
Each bloody celebrant;
Caught as in a painting . . . lips about to speak:
She who had so many times
Shed luster on them at her father's feasts,
Singing with her lucent voice—
Tender, virginal—
The hymn of grace at the third salute.

[CLYTEMNESTRA *has reentered and stands listening, attended by her women*]

Antistrophe 6

I did not see the sequel, nor can tell it:
The crafts of Calchas never fail.
And Justice so designs
That only those who suffer learn. . . . But let that go;
You'll meet it when it comes; don't seize
On trouble: it will break with the morning's rays.
God send us something better now,
As this single-minded watcher hopes—

The close fence of our realm.[8]

[LEADER [9] *of the* CHORUS
turns to the queen]

I wait upon your royalty, Clytemnestra:
Obeisance most fitting to our master's queen
Now the kingly throne stands tenantless.
Is it good and certain news you have
Or only wished-for thinking with your sacrifice?
With all respect to reticence, I'd gladly know.

CLYTEMNESTRA

News, sir, as blessed as the proverbial dawn
Which springs in gladness from her mother Night.
Listen to a greater joy than you could hope to learn:
Priam's city has fallen to the Argive might.[10]

CHORUS *and* CLYTEMNESTRA

CH: What did you say? It escapes belief.

CL: The Greeks have taken Troy. Am I plain enough?

CH: Happiness suffuses me, summoning my tears.

CL: Yes, your eyes give you away—your loyal heart.

CH: But have you proof? Is there evidence?

CL: Proof? Why not? Unless some god has cheated us.

CH: Or unless you are the victim of a dream.

CL: I don't take revelations from a dormant brain.

CH: Perhaps a rumor, then, buoyed up your hopes?

CL: You treat me like some young and silly girl.

8 These two lines refer to Clytemnestra: they are veiled, ironic,
sarcastic, and slightly sinister. The Greek word ἕρκος, which I have
translated as "fence," can also mean "net" and "noose."
9 It is to be taken for granted that "Chorus" means "Leader of
the Chorus" whenever this embarks on dialogue.
10 In the Greek these four lines are, prosodically, typical of the way
Aeschylus often coordinates the sound of his end syllables with
assonance, consonance, rhyme and near rhyme. They are typical,
too, of the way I have handled the more obvious of such passages.

CH: But when—what time please—did the city fall?

CL: This very night, as I have said, which bore this
                                                glorious day.

CH: But who could ever carry news so fast?

CLYTEMNESTRA

Hephaestus, god of fire—
Flashing it from Ida in a blaze.
Beacon after beacon in courier flame posting here:
Ida to the Hermian head of Lemnos, then
Across the island its great beam caught
By the crag of Athos—Zeus's crag.
And with a leapfrog over the sea
The strong light skipped with joy:
Tipping his firebrand golden message like the sun
Onto the watchtowers of Macistus, who,
Not slow nor sluggard caught asleep
But perfect messenger in turn,
Streamed the signal onwards far
Beyond the banks of the Euripus
To the lookout at Mesapion, who blazed
An answer from their brittle pile
Of tindered heather—touched their fire riders on.
It mustered strength:
There was no waning in that fire's leap
Across the plain of Asopus.
It bounded like the coruscating moon
To the scaur of Citheron—
Striking forth another running flame.
And in welcome to that far-sent light
They fanned a blaze that went beyond all bidding:
It broke across the lake of Gorgopis and shone
High on Aegyplanctus' mountaintop,
Exacting there immediate rage for fire.
Then, richly heaped,
It waxed into a full beard of flame
Sent searing past the bluff that lowers
Over the Saronic frith, until

It streaked upon the Spider's Rock of Arachnus,
Our nearest beacon hill.
And here it pitched—the roof of the Atreidae—
No upstart flame from Ida's pedigree.

Such was the course my fire-runners ran:
Relay on to relay, finishing their chain.
The final sprinter first and last has won.
And such the warrant that I give to you in token
That to me from Troy my lord has spoken.[11]

CHORUS

The gods be praised at once, my queen!
But words so full of wonder make me keen
To hear it end to end, so speak again.

CLYTEMNESTRA

The Greeks have Troy this day.
Oh, I think I hear unmingling clamors rise:
You'd hardly say that vinegar and oil
Mix lovingly together in a bowl!
Defeat and Triumph are in the air,
With different cries:
A double consequence to hear.
Great wailing first, from lips no longer free;
A fastening on corpses: husbands, brothers,
Children on old parents—dear ones dead.
Whilst *there* a night of battle turmoil sets
The flagging soldiers down with famishing
For any breakfast that the town can give:
Discipline forgotten, all pell mell,
Each one grabbing at his private luck.
Ensconced already in sequestered Trojan homes
And saved from frosts and dews beneath the sky,
Now they are men of sweetened luck and they will sleep
Unsentineled the sweet night through.

---

[11] These five lines and the three following are again a strong example
of the way Aeschylus dovetails the sound pattern of his line endings.
Here he gives these final syllables: nomoi—menoi—ōn—ō—omoi—
omai—asai—in.

If they will use with due regard the city's gods
(The conquered country's godly shrines),
The spoilers' turn will never turn to spoiled.
But woe to any premature and insensate excess:
The army both assaulted and upset by greed! . . .
There still remains the other half to go
Of their voyage and their run to safety home.
And even if nothing untoward befalls
And in pious blamelessness they come their way—
The curses of the dead still lie awake.

You've been listening to a woman's words . . .
But may the good prevail—come shining clear;
For in this course I've put my heart's desire.

CHORUS

Spoken, Lady, like a sound and solid man.
Your evidence convinces me
And I must turn to glorify the gods:
No ungreat cause is won from our great sacrifice.

[CLYTEMNESTRA *goes into the palace with her attendants.
The* CHORUS *regroups and the old men sing of thanksgiving, the sin of pride, the cruelty of war*]

CHORUS

Second Stasimon

O Zeus our king and lovely Night
Caparisoned with victory,
Who on the Trojan towers threw
A mesh and hood that no one could—
Nor great nor small—leap high enough
    Or wide away
From huge enthrall of universal doom:
    Great god of guests so I praise you.
    These things you did and long ago
    You aimed at Paris, bent your bow
    Never to shoot short of the mark
        Nor idly past the stars.

Strophe 1

The "Stroke of God" it must be called:
  Every trace there of his hand.
He wills and it is done. A fool hath said
That Heaven has no care when mortal men
Trample down the sanctities. He was not wise.
      Oh it stands revealed:
      More abundant ruin
Than all the lush excess their house can hold
    And all the sniffing arrogance
      Of their surpassing pride.
      Let riches be discreet,
      Sufficiency suffice;
      Oh let a man be sound.
      It is no bulwark wealth
      To save the greedy heart
From spurning out of sight the mighty seat
        Of Righteousness.

Antistrophe 1

Beaten forward by Obsession
    (Monstrous child of brooding Havoc):
All remedy in vain—he has no cover
For his sin; it casts its evil gleam
    Like brass adulterate gone black
        Through touch and wear . . .
      A boy to chase a bird,
      Oh—wild—winging!
And brand inveterate a city's name.
    No god to hear his pleading
      But rather sweep away
      The sinner of such sins.
      And so did Paris come
      To the palace of the sons
      Of Atreus; profaned
The board and courtesy of friend
        And rapt a wife.

Strophe 2

Her citizens in shields, she left behind
    A stridency of spears,
      The heavy clang of ships,
And Ilium dealt a deathblow not a dower.
Oh, what a wanton tripping through the gates!
The stricken comments of the palace bards:
"My house! my house! my desolated masters!
Poor amorous bed indented with their love!
Poor husband mute, dishonored, never damning,
    Never dreaming that she'd gone;
      His seawards longing eyes have seemed
To frame her phantom ordering the house. The grace
      Of her sweet statues now
        A curse to him:
      For, in their starveling gaze
      Everything is drained
        Of Aphrodite."

Antistrophe 2

    Dream forms in forlorn procession bring
      Him vain delight . . . O,
    Vanity of blessed visions!
Wafted down the avenues of sleep;
Slipping through the hands and vanishing.
Is sorrow *this* which strikes at hearth and home?
This is nothing next to other sorrows still.
O universal sad property of death!
Owned in every home of that great company
      Which said good-bye to Greece;
    There is too much to touch the heart.
For did you send a man away—a man you knew?—
      Urns and ashes come back home,
        No living man.

Strophe 3

For the War-god barters bodies with his gold.
    On a spear point balances their worth

In battle. Straight from Troy,
Fired, full-weighted, wet
With tears and neatly packed
In jars, he sends their friends
        The price of man:
    A bitter residue of dust.
    Then pathetic epitaphs:
        This one "skilled in combat,"
    That one "nobly killed in action" . . .
    "For another's wife," some whisper.
And so regret, reproach, come creeping on
Towards the House of Atreus—these quarrelers.
    While there beneath the walls of Ilium
    Those others in their splendid bodies lie:
    Conquerors, but covered and entombed
        In soil they loathed.

Antistrophe 3

There's danger in the grumblings of a people's ire.
    It ratifies a nation in its curse.
        Some night-swathed thing
        Waits upon my ear.
        The gods have eyes:
    The multimurderer is marked,
        And in the end
    The black Fates overturn and batter down
    The lucky but too lawless man—
        His life a shadow
Where arrivals in oblivion are most lame.
    Overreaching glory is a ruin.
    The flashing glance of Zeus consumes the proud.
    I'll have no happiness that challenges;
        Be sacker of no cities nor
        Ever live to see my soul
            In turn despoiled,
            Another's slave.[12]

---

[12] The time taken by this long choral ode represents dramatically that several days have passed since the news of Troy's downfall first arrived; otherwise the Herald announces Agamemnon much

AN ELDER

A beacon's brought exciting news.
A rumor's sweeping all the town.
But is it certain? Who can tell?
Or only gossip god-inspired?

ANOTHER

Well, who's so infantile or fatuous
He'd let a newsy bonfire set his heart ablaze
And then collapse at shift of it.

ANOTHER

Just like a woman—before the proof—
To lap up what she wants to hear.

ANOTHER

A woman's mind is all too ready made.
A woman's word emblazoning renown
Is all too ready rubbish.

LEADER OF THE CHORUS

We shall know in a moment about these flaring lights,
These running relays of beacon fires:
Whether there's any truth in them at all
Or whether this lightsome luminary
Hasn't ridden in upon a dream
And cast a spell on us and made us fools—
For look: I see a herald from the shore,
His forehead shaded with an olive crown;
Dust and mud (its sisterly and thirsty friend)
Tell me that no dumb charades
Or smoking bonfires sparked upon the hills
Are going to signal us, but good plain words:

---

too soon. It is typical, however, of Aeschylus's sense of time that
he regards the two events as almost simultaneous. It is not the
temporal sequence that is important to him, but the causal and
dramatic.

To make us either celebrate or else . . .
No. I'll not accept the opposite.
The news was good and may we better it.

ANOTHER ELDER

If any call down any less on this our city,
Let him reap the rotten fruit of his perversity!

[*A* HERALD *enters: a remnant of the returning Greek armies. He shows by his old and dirty uniform that he has recently been through a great deal*]

HERALD

O soil of my fathers! Happy land!
The one bright spot come true in all ten years
Of hopes in shreds—
I never dared to dream
That on this ground of Argos here I'd die:
My own, my special plot.
You blessed earth! You blessed light and sun!
And Zeus supreme
Lord of the land!
And you great god of Delphi too
(Only shoot no more your darts at us—
You were implacable enough on Scamander's banks):
Be our healer, Lord Apollo, and preserver.
Praise
Be every god of battle.
Hermes, sweet herald—
You favorite of all heralds!
And you our hero ancestors
Who cheered our army to the wars,
Now welcome home
The remnant which the wars have spared.

Come, palaces of kings and roofs beloved:
You solemn judgment seats and deities that front
the sun,
Bright-eyed today if ever—
Radiantly receive your lord, so long gone.

For like a light, beatifically he comes
To you, to all of you: great Agamemnon King.

Render him the welcome he deserves.
Troy he's toppled down; plowed up her plain
With God's own mattock, Zeus the Punisher's.
Her divinities, her shrines, her altars gone;
Uprooted all her country's seed—erased.
Such is the yoke he's thrown around the neck of Troy:
This king,
First son of Atreus,
This man of triumph.
He comes worthy of honor beyond all living men.
Paris and his guilty city cannot say
Their sin was worth their suffering.
Bound over in a suit for rape and robbery,
He's lost his surety and broken down
His father's house: the very ground it stood.
Twice the price have Priam's sons
Made in payment for their sins.

CHORUS *and* HERALD

CH: Herald from the Greek battalions, we welcome
     you.

HR: Oh welcome! . . . even to death, if the gods so
     wished.

CH: Were you very heartsick then for home?

HR: Enough to brim my eyes with tears of happiness.

CH: It was a sweet sickness then that struck you down.

HR: How so? Explain your drift.

CH: To love and long and in return be loved.

HR: You mean, the land we longed for longed for us?

CH: From out of the depths we often groaned.

HR: Why so oppressed? Such melancholy?

CH: I've learned that . . . silence is the only safe receipt.

HR: What's that? You went in fear of someone, with our prince away?

CH: As you said just now: enough to welcome death.

HERALD

Ah! but it's well and done with now.
Yes, it's been a mixed experience all these years:
Success and failure—one might say—half-and-half
                                        composed. . . .
But who except a god expects to have it all one way?

If I should tell you of our miseries:
Overcrowded decks and quarters cramped,
Narrow berths—our daily fare . . . Ah, then!
What was there *not* to complain about?
And once we'd landed—more abominations still:
Beds in the open underneath their hostile walls,
Constant drizzle from above,
Drenching meadow dews beneath—
Rotting our uniforms,
Tangling lice into our hair.

Then the winters—you've no idea!
A cold to kill birds dead;
And Ida's snows—
Enough to make one shudder!
Or the sweltering summers: the noonday sea—
Not a wave, not a breath,
Upon its flaccid slumbering.

But why complain?
It's done with now.
The dead are done with too!
They'll never want to rise and live again.
What's the point of calling out the roll? The point
Of crying over life's unkindnesses?
Pack up your troubles, so say I—the lot of them.
After all,
For us Argive soldiers who are left,

Our losses do not balance out our gains.
We have every right in the full face of this day's sun,
As we scud across the land and sea,
To trumpet forth our boast:
  "The Argive host in time took Troy,
And in the dwellings of the gods of Greece
They nailed up these: the prize of ancient days and joy."

  Hear it, then,
And sing our captains' praises and our city's.
Give thanks to Zeus for what he's won. . . .
My speech is done.

CHORUS

A speech which overwhelms—has no rebuff.
Ah! Age is always young enough to learn. . . .
But here is news which mostly must concern
Clytemnestra and the palace, though it makes me rich
                                                    enough.

[CLYTEMNESTRA *enters while the* LEADER *is speaking*]

CLYTEMNESTRA

My shout of joy I sent up long ago:
The moment those first messengers of fire
Came streaming through the night,
Blazing forth the fall and waste of Ilium.
Then some sniggering person said:
  "Bonfires! And great Troy destroyed?
You credit *that?*
How like a woman's hysterical credulity!"

  They made me out a wandering fool;
But even so I went on with my sacrifice.
And soon in every part, in every corner of the town,
Everyone—just like a woman, ha!—
Hymned and shouted out his paeans of gratitude.
And in the temples of the gods
The spice-fed flames were soothed

And incense fumed.[13]

But now, what need for you to tell the whole long thing
When I can get it, every word, from the man himself the
                                                          king?
The finest welcome that I can—
My famous husband coming back!—is my design.
For what sweeter vision for a woman:
The gates unbarred, her man returned—
Safe from the wars by the grace of God?

So go and tell my husband this:
"Hurry home, you darling of the town.
Home to a wife that's waiting
Faithful as you left her,
Your own sweet palace watchdog,
Fierce to those who hate you;
Oh, altogether one who kept the seal intact
In all these years:
Who knows no more of tampering with other men
Or breath of shame
Than stains know virgin bronze."

[CLYTEMNESTRA *leaves*]

HERALD

Highflung words indeed—
If not freighted with the truth
And proper to a highborn lady's mouth.

CHORUS

That's the way she wants her words to go:
A most persuasive speech if your ears are clear.
But tell me, Herald, what of Menelaus?
Is *he* back too, safe and sound with you—
This country's much-loved prince?

[13] One must remember that the smoke of incense goes up only
when the flames die down and the grains begin to smolder.

HERALD *and* CHORUS

HR: I know no way to make a falsehood fair
and keep it so for long my friends.

CH: Or any way to give fair news which yet is true?
Fair torn from foul can never hide.

HR: He vanished from the Argive fleet,
man and ship. I speak the truth.

CH: Did he set out in sight of all from Troy?
Or did a storm strike one and all and snatch him
from the fleet?

HR: Bowman, you have hit the bull's-eye straight!
The whole sorry business in a phrase.

CH: But when the rumor reached you from the fleet,
Was it that he'd perished or was still alive?

HR: No one knows. There's none can make that clear,
Save the great Sun alone who warms the earth to life.

CH: Would you say this storm that broke upon the ships
came from some god's anger? How did it end?

HERALD

Oh, do not stain this happy day
With a bulletin that's black.
Keep praise and tears apart for different gods.
When a messenger with deadly face
Arrives to tell his town the dreadful fact:
A military collapse,
A knockout blow to all the state;
And Ares with his double whip—
Double-deadly favorite, twice bloody pair
Multiplies his victims, multiplies his gutted homes . . .
When a messenger, I say,
Crammed with such disaster comes—
Then is the time to shriek to hell and not to heaven.
But when one comes announcing to a cheering city
News of some resounding coup—

Is that the time to mix calamity with triumph
And blurt it out:
  "A storm has hit the Greeks: one god-inspired"?

   Yes, fire and sea, those old antagonists,
Have made a pact; have ratified their bond;
Have smashed into the Argive ships of line . . .
In the night:
Ill-waved evil running high;
A Thracian gale;
Ships thrashing into ships—
Bucking and butting in the hurricane,
Stampeding into mists of storm and thundering rain:
A panic shepherding towards oblivion.
And then the sun's rays lighting up the scene:
The wide Aegean flowered with the Argive dead,
And flotsam everywhere.

   As for us, some god, no human hand,
Kept touch upon the tiller, stole or begged us off,
And brought our vessel out with not a timber sprung.
Some rescuing spirit must have willed to sit inside our ship
And stop her from succumbing to that smash and flood
                              of surf
Or grinding on the stony shoals.
And we the refugees from that death-sea hell,
When the white dawn broke,
Could not convince ourselves we lived—our luck.
Our thoughts were heavy with the all-too-fresh ordeal:
The finished and the beaten fleet.
So if there's life in any of them yet,
Now they must be saying we're dead—why not?
Just as we think the very same of them.

   Well, may the best work out!
Menelaus first, especially him—oh, he'll come back,
If the sun's rays anywhere can spot him out:
Alive still, light in his eyes, by Zeus' design,
Who surely never would annihilate our race—
There's hope that he'll come home again. . . .

You've heard. Be sure you've heard the truth.

[*The* HERALD *goes out.*[14] *The* CHORUS, *now alone, takes up the theme of* HELEN's *sin and the sufferings that await all unbridled self-seeking*]

CHORUS

Strophe 1—Third Stasimon

Who was the man that gave the name
So absolutely apposite?
Surely someone *we* can't see,
Shaping his tongue to destiny
And styling her by prophecy?
Helen the War-wooer! Source of Strife!
True to her name:[15] hell for the ships!
Man's hell and the city's hell—
Sailing away from her dainty boudoir's
    Opulent drapings;
Breathed onwards by Zephyr the giant,
    With men-of-war many-manned chasing
    The wake and the ghost of the oarblades;
    Then running their boats up the river
    Simois' shaded strands . . .
    The battle of blood for love.

Antistrophe 1

Ilium had a wedding-death
Titled by its proper name,
Consummated well by Wrath:
Paying cuckold host his long
Debt and Zeus-presiding's song—
    Oh too loud!—for the bride;
    And the kin of the bridegroom, who sang

14 The number of actors in a Greek play was strictly limited. The actor who played the part of the Herald now goes off to dress for the part (probably) of Agamemnon.
15 A play on the name: ἑλένας (*helenas*) means "ship-destroying." ἑλεῖν (*helein*) means to "destroy," "quell," "seize," "abduct," "seduce."

            The wedding march.
            But the music has changed in the town:
            Ancient city of Priam ...
            Weeping and gnashing of teeth
            For Paris embedded with Death;
            Life of so many laments
            For all those slaughtered sons:[16]
            Desolate tears and blood.

                        Strophe 2

        A man once reared a lion cub
        In his house, a tender thing
        Taken from its mother's milk,
        Gentle at its dawn of life:
            Sweet little pet of the children,
            Charming to the aged.
        Much was it held in people's arms,
        Dandled like a human child,
        Fawning on the hand that fed it:
            Bright-eyed for its belly.

                        Antistrophe 2

        Then one day the lion cub
        Showed its proper parentage:
        Gave its thanks for being raised,
        At a banquet never bidden ...
            Running amuck in the sheep,
            Bloodying the house
        Caught in helpless tragedy;
        Turned it into a charnel house:
        A fiendish priest by the wrath of God
            Pampered in the home.

                        Strophe 3

        So once there came to the town of Troy
        What seemed a very breath of calm:

---

[16] Priam, king of Troy, had fifty sons and twelve daughters (one of whom was Cassandra).

Unruffled, delicate,
Rare as a jewel is rich and rare;
Doe-eyed dartlings from her eyes;
Flower to prick the hand with longing.
Then suddenly she wheeled around,
Did her wedding to the death—
Evil guest and evil comrade—
    Burst on Priam's children
    Like a demon: bridal
    Tears at Zeus' reception.

Antistrophe 3

It hath been said of old by men:
Prosperity becomes mature,
Grows great with child,
Engenders it and cannot die
Until it does. A man's success
Breeds in his house a hungry brood
Of rapacious miseries.
But *I* say this—not like the rest—
It is the *act* of wickedness
    Bears wickedness just like it.
    A pious house begets
    Fair piety.

Strophe 4

Sooner or later Pride-
The-Old makes Pride-the-New,
Sporting in the wicked
(When its birth is due)
    A frenzied thing:
Infatuate, unwholesome, strong,
Insatiate, obsessive, black
    Curse upon the house—
    Image of its parents.

Antistrophe 4

But Goodness is a lamp

That shines in smoky homes
And honors him that's just.
From golden mansions, dirty
    Hands, she turns,
Looking away, to the pure of home.
She has no awe of power or wealth
    Or counterfeited fame;
    But orders all things well.

[AGAMEMNON *in a chariot with* CASSANDRA *beside him
(but hidden from view) enters with soldiers bearing
trophies, and a numerous retinue. The* CHORUS *sings its
welcome*]

CHORUS

Welcome, great King, stormer of Troy,
    True son of Atreus.
How shall I greet you? How shall I honor you?
Not overstepping, not underscoring
    The appropriate praises.
Too many people favor appearances
    And offend what is right.
Everyone's ready to sigh for the stricken,
    But the pang and the sorrow
    Never goes through to the heart.
Show them rejoicers: they take on rejoicing,
    Forcing their faces to smile.
But the good shepherd knows his sheep
And never mistakes the eyes of a man
    Who is fraud when he seems to be friend
    And cheats with his watery fondness.

Even you—let me tell you—equipping your army
Hot after Helen, for me were depicted
    Once in very poor colors:
Not steering aright your rudder of reason;
Conjuring up courage for men who were dying,
    By the blood of a sacrifice.[17]

---

[17] The criminal sacrifice of Iphigenia.

But now from my heart not lightly nor loveless,
"Welcome!" I say on work well done.
In the course of time you will learn by inquiring
Which were the honest ones, which the dishonorable
    Citizens guarding the city.

[AGAMEMNON *replies from
the chariot*]

AGAMEMNON

First, Argos, you—
Most fittingly I greet:
You and your incumbent deities,
Joint authors of my safe return,
Who rendered me my vengeance over Priam's town.

For, oh yes, the gods to every spoken plea turned deaf;
Cast their ballots in the urn for blood
Unanimously—
The wholesale sack of Troy.
To the opposite urn came only Hope;
Hung her hand, dropped nothing in.
Smoke still marks the city's fall.
A wreath of havoc breathes there still
Among the dying ashes:
The fat reek of wealth.

For this success we owe the gods
Some memorable return . . .
A city netted in our noose of hate,
Ground down to powder for a woman
By the Beast of Argos—Wooden Horse—
Spawning its teeming panoply,
Springing its leap beneath the setting Pleiades.[18]
Over the ramparts the ravening lion
Bounded to his kill
And lapped king's blood.

[CLYTEMNESTRA *enters with her train of attendants carry-*

18 I.e., toward the end of autumn.

*ing rich purple tapestries. She halts at the top of the steps
and listens*]

This to the gods: a preamble of thanksgiving.
Now for those sentiments of yours still ringing in my ears.
I say as you (I am your ally there):
How few there are whose natures feel no gall
At a friend's prosperity!
For envy settles like a poison on the heart;
Doubles the load of a man's disease:
His own soul's pain
And the pain of another's happiness.
I speak with cause—I know it well—
The sham reflection in the glass,
A shadow's shade:
Those so flamboyant seemers—oh, to dote on me.
Only Odysseus, setting sail against his will,
Was hitched with me and hitched to loyalty. . . .
Be he live or dead, I'll say it of him still.

For the rest,
As concerns this city and its gods:
We shall deliberate in full and public session.
Where all goes well
We shall arrange that well it so continues.
Where doctoring and remedies are needed
We shall with all humane intent,
With cautery or knife,
Try to stem the sad contagion.

And now to my halls and palace hearth,
Where the gods shall be saluted first.
They sped me out; they brought me home.
Come, Victory, attend!
Befriend me to the end.

[CLYTEMNESTRA *walks
down the steps*]

CLYTEMNESTRA

Sirs, good citizens, grave elders of the state,
I am not ashamed to let you see

How I hold him in my heart. . . .
Such shyness wears away in time.
I tell no lesson learned from others:
My own unhappy life for all those years
With him away beneath the walls of Troy.

　　First, how cruel it is:
A woman sits at home,
Torn from her man—
Desolate,
The prey of every frightening report.
A messenger comes in . . .
Hot on his heels another
With news that's worse.
Grief and uproar in the house.

　　Had my husband here been wounded with as many
　　　　　　　　　　　　　　　　　　　　　wounds
As have spouted rumors from these walls,
He would be gashed more full of holes than any net.
Had he died as many deaths as legend said,
He might have been Geryon's double with three bodies,
Each one mantled with three copious mounds,[19]
Dying once for each.
Many a time have vicious tales like these
Made others hold me down
And loose the long high-dangling rope
Cast around my neck.
That is why our son, the symbol of our faith,
Yours and mine,
Is not standing here as stand he should—
Our son, Orestes.
But do not wonder:
Strophius the Phocian, our kind ally,
Has him in his care,
Forewarning me of the double risk we ran:
Your jeopardy beneath the walls of Troy,
And the chance of riot at home;

[19] With Schütz I omit the dubious and awkward line 871 (in the
Loeb Classics edition).

For it is born to man to hit the man that's down. . . .
This is no specious apology.

    As for myself,
The wellsprings of my tears are dry;
Not a drop is left.
My eyes are sore with watching late at nights,
Weeping for those bonfires set for you but never lit.
And if I drowsed I dreamt of you;
Wakened by the gnat's thin airy whine—
Saw you in such sorrows still
As far outstretched that little space of sleep.

    But now, all is endured.
With a mind released I salute this man:
The watchdog of the fold,
Sure forestay of the ship,
Fundamental pillar of the palace beams,
A father's only son,
Sight of land to sailors past all hope,
First fair day when the tempest's done,
Parched traveler's living rill,
And now: most sweet escape from doom.
Such the epithets I dare to call him by.
May Envy keep away—
We've paid her many times before this day.

    And now, my lord, dear head, come down.
Step from your car;
But not upon our common earth:
Not the foot, my king, that trod down Troy.

    Women, to your task. Why do you wait?
Spread out the tapestries before his walk.
The purple [20] path at once strew down.
Let holy Recompense escort him to his unexpected home.
The rest, my diligence, which does not sleep,
Shall by the grace of God, due orders keep.

---

[20] Some scholars argue that the Greek πορφύρα (*porphura*) was probably nearer crimson. However, the "royal purple" is what it has been throughout English literature and I prefer not to throw away the garnered connotations of our tongue.

[*The women begin to spread out rich carpetings between the chariot and the palace*]

AGAMEMNON

   Daughter of Leda, guardian of my house,
Well suited to my absence is your speech:
Long drawn out.
Praise from another would be more appropriate.
Besides, I need no woman's coddling,
No barbarian display,
With groveling on the ground and gaping praise;
Or have my path decked out to catch the Evil Eye
With carpets and embroiderings.
Keep these things and all the glory of them for the gods.
To walk on furbished trappings is for me, mere man,
A most disturbing thing.
Respect me as a man and not a god.
I need no footmats and no fripperies to sound my fame.
God's greatest gift is to keep us from our follies;
And happy alone is he who ends his life still happily.
If I go on as I am, there is good hope for me.

CLYTEMNESTRA *and* AGAMEMNON

CL: You mean you would upset this plan of mine?

AG: I only mean, be sure, I shall not upset mine.

CL: You must have vowed to act like this through fear.

AG: No man ever meant more fully what he said.

CL: But what would Priam have done, d'you think, if
                             he had won?

AG: Gone stalking down the tapestries, I do believe.

CL: Then don't allow mere fear of man to hinder you.

AG: Public opinion is a power, my dear, to reckon with.

CL   Perhaps, but where no envy, there no admiration is.

AG: This lust for battle hardly suits a woman.

CL: But even losing suits a mighty man.

AG: Is this the kind of war you want to win?

CL: Oh please! If you'll just let your triumph stoop to
                                                    mine.

AGAMEMNON

Well, if you must . . . be quick.
Have someone loose my boots—
Those stalwart servants of my treading feet.
I want no far-off beam from some god's eye
To smite me as I trample on these deep-sea purples.[21]
Crass waste it is for tramping feet
To mar such substance and such stuffs that silver bought.

[*A slave comes forward and undoes his boots.* AGAMEM-
NON *steps to the ground and in so doing reveals* CASSAN-
DRA *huddled in the chariot*]

So much for that. . . . And now,
Show some kindness to this foreign girl and take her in.
God's eyes shine clemently from far
On clemency in power;
And no one freely harnesses
Himself to slavery.
She came with me, choice flower:
Prize of an empire, present of an army.

So, overborne by you, I shall proceed
To tread the purple to my palace halls.

[AGAMEMNON *continues to
stand where he is*]

CLYTEMNESTRA

There is the sea—
And who shall drain it dry?
Vast factory of purple drops

---

[21] The famous Tyrian purple was made from creatures of the sea—
mollusks.

And every spill of it worth silver:
Inexhaustible treasury of royal dye.
Your house is stuffed with these,
God's ample benisons—
Not a room goes bare.
I should have vowed a hundred tapestries
To be trampled on—if oracles had asked—
When I went to bargain for your life.

When a root still lives
It sends the umbrage of its leaves
To envelop with a greeny bower
The house against the dogdays' glare.
You, returning to your hearth and home,
Are like a fire in winter time;
Or the grapes' sweet turning (by Zeus' design)
From sourness into wine,
When the master of the house comes home:
Bringing coolness into every room.

[AGAMEMNON *begins to walk down the carpet as* CLYTEMNESTRA *watches him*]

Zeus, O Zeus! who consummates:
Consummate my prayers.
Your providence provide
Consummation of these cares!

[CLYTEMNESTRA *follows into the palace.* CASSANDRA *is left with the* ELDERS, *who sing ominously of coming dissolution*]

CHORUS

Strophe 1—Fourth Stasimon

What beats against my heart like dread?
Prophetic, calculated, grim?
Chants unbiddenly, unbought?
In my bosom hope vacates
    Her throne. No confidence
Can overturn this nightmare of no meaning.
        And—long since—

Time in the sandbank shallows heaps
The anchors of the ships of line:
  Held from their flight
    To Ilium.

Antistrophe 1

I saw them coming back myself:[22]
My own eyes made it clear—and yet
I cannot stop my soul which sings,
Self-aware and deep, a song:
  Epicedial, lyreless,
Furies' dirge; . . . powerless to hold again
  My old strong hope.
It is no fantasy, these fears,
But spasmic, real, from a breast-struck h eart.
  Oh, could they fade, be false,
    Be not fulfilled!

Strophe 2

Rude is the lusty thrust of health
Pressing its bounds with greedy strengt h
As if no sickness were next door
  With but a thin partition.
So does human happiness
Pressing onwards on its course
Suddenly break on the unseen reef.
If only caution with a measured cast
  Would jettison a little wealth
    Garnered in the hold,
The doom-weighted edifice would not be swamped,
      Would not go down.
  And Zeus in generous providence
  Would from the plowshare's yearly yield
    Set plague and famine back.

22 Agamemnon and his army.

Antistrophe 2

Once the death-shed blood of man
Speckles the ground, what spell of charms
Can sing it back? When even one [23]
   So privy to the skill
Of raising dead, great Zeus cut down
To warn us. . . . Yet if the gods did not
Arrange the play of fate on fate
To cancel out an overload of pain,
   My heart would now have overrun
     The torrents of my tongue.
But still beneath the gloom my spirit moans—
     Lost and in pain,
   Hopeless of unraveling ever
   Some happiness of grace in time:
     My soul in flame.

[*Toward the end of this choral song* CLYTEMNESTRA *has entered. She looks challengingly at* CASSANDRA *still sitting motionless in the chariot with her prophet's wand in her hand and wearing fillets around her hair*]

CLYTEMNESTRA

Inside the house, Cassandra—I mean you too.
Zeus has been kind to let you share our rituals here,
Where you may take your place among the many slaves
At the altar of our presiding god.
Down from the car. And no pride please!
Even Alcmena's son,[24] so they say,
Once had to face being sold—
To eat the bread of slavery.
If the experience is thrust upon you
At least you have the luck of masters old to money.
The newly rich with unexpected wealth

---

[23] Asclepius, whom Zeus struck with lightning for raising Hippolytus to life.
[24] Heracles—sold as a slave to Omphale, queen of Lydia: (because of his murder of Iphitus).

Are cruel to their slaves beyond all decency.
From us you can expect only what is proper.

[CASSANDRA *still sits motionless*]

CHORUS

She is talking to you, Cassandra,
And she is being explicit.
You will obey her, won't you—
Caught as you are by Fate?
Will you . . . won't you?

CLYTEMNESTRA

Perhaps she only understands some outlandish twittering,
Like a swallow. I shall have to speak within her wits
To make my point.

CHORUS

Go, Cassandra: she offers you your only choice.
Please leave the chariot seat.

CLYTEMNESTRA

I simply have no time
To dawdle with this woman here outside the door.
The victims stand already at the hearthstone for the
                                                    kill—
An act of grace we never hoped to make.
So, if you're going to join in it, don't dally;
Or if you fail to follow what I mean,
Instead of words make signs with your barbarian hand.

[CASSANDRA *shudders but says nothing*]

CHORUS

Madam, she is a foreigner,
She needs a good interpreter.
Why, she's like some freshly captured animal!

CLYTEMNESTRA

Mad—I say. Quite!
Cocking her inward ear to something crazed:
Fresh from a captured city.
She'll foam and bleed at the mouth,
Play her passions out
Before she ever takes the bit.
Well, I'm not waiting—
For insolence and waste of breath.

[CLYTEMNESTRA *exits, sweeping through the palace doors.*
The old men turn to CASSANDRA *again*]

CHORUS

I can't lose my temper too: I pity her.
Come, poor girl— leave that forlorn carriage.
Give way to what must be: your unfamiliar yoke.

CASSANDRA *and* CHORUS

CA: Oh, the hue and the cry!
     Apollo! Apollo!

CH: Apollo—why?
     He's not the god of those who cry.

CA: Oh, the hue and the cry!
     Apollo! Apollo!

CH: Apollo again? A most sinister shout!
     A god who has no place with wailing.

CA: Apollo! Apollo!
     Guiding god [25] . . . oh, me to death!
     This time to death appalling.

---

[25] Cassandra stares at the image of "Apollo of the Paths" which stood
outside the street door of every house. . . . I have tried to retain some
semblance of the Greek play on words, which run (line 1080):
Appollon Apollon / aguiat, appollōn emos / apōlesas, etc. Ἄπολλον
Ἄπολλον / ἀγυιᾶτ ἀπόλλων ἐμός / ἀπώλεσας κτλ. Here ἀπόλλων and
ἀπώλεσας are parts of the verb ἀπόλλυμι, which means "to destroy."

CH: I think she's going to prophesy her own disaster.
Even in a slave the gift divine endures.

CA: Apollo! Apollo!
Guiding god . . . oh, me to death!
What house? Oh where have you guided?

CHORUS

To the house of Atreus. Did you not know?
I tell you so: you will not find it false.

CASSANDRA

No no: to a house God hates,
Full of family butcheries:
Dangling with horrors;
Human slaughterhouse . . .
The seeping floor.

CHORUS

She seems to have a bloodhound's nose, this foreigner.
She is on the scent that leads to blood.

CASSANDRA

Yes! Hot on the clues—my certain clues:
That screaming of children there;
Carving of babies' flesh—
Festal roasts for a father's feasting.

CHORUS

We have heard of your power to read the future.
But there is no demand for prophets here.

CASSANDRA

[*Pointing wildly to behind
the closed doors of the palace*]

The plotter, what? . . .

Ah! what's she plot?
What novelty of hideousness and hideous crime?
Schemed in there—
Beyond all salvage,
Beyond love's saving;
While help stands off?

CHORUS

These prophecies mean nothing to me.
Those others do: the city shrieks with children's cries.

CASSANDRA

You wretched woman! So you'll do it?
Your husband bridegroomed from his bath . . .
Shall I tell it—how? . . . the end:
So quickly now . . . a hand
To grope . . . a hand to strike.

CHORUS

It still means nothing to me.
Riddles first and now black oracles.

CASSANDRA

No, no, don't you see it?
A death-net? Yes, a snare . . . No, *she's* the snare,
Casting bed and murder into one.
Yell it to mankind ye intemperate pack:
A victim downed!

CHORUS

What spirit of damnation do you summon up
To howl upon this haunted house?
Your voices chill. My blood runs pale:
Back to the heart each pallid drop;
An inward dripping like a mortal wound
Ebbing as the rays of life go down—
And death comes quick.

CASSANDRA

There! There! See it now?
Separate the bull from cow.
She has him tangled in his robe.
With the black trick of her horn,
    She lunges:
    He crumples
  Into the brimful tub.
Oh, murder and swindle! I say,
    In a bath.

CHORUS

I could never boast of cleverness at oracles
  But these spell something rotten out.
  Did blessing ever come to man
    Through oracles?
  No, it is a dangerous art:
    Chants horrors forth
    In multiples.

CASSANDRA

Pity me! Pity! My own turn now:
Affliction in the bitter cup—
  Lamentation . . . mine.
So unblessedly you bring me here:
    For what?
Only to die; conjoined in death:
    How not?

CHORUS

Poor craze-tossed sybil in a trance!
Unstopping music of your fate:
You melancholy nightingale,
  Untuned brown bird,
Breaking forth with "Itys! Itys!"[26]

---

[26] Onomatopeia, and also the name of Philomela's nephew, whom she lamented after being changed into a nightingale. She had been raped by Tereus, her brother-in-law.

Through the thicket
Of a broken heart and ruined days.

CASSANDRA

Oh, for the nightingale—her so mellifluous lot!
Invested with a feathered form divine:
A sweet life free from all lament.
But me, for me, there hangs
The double-headed ax.

CHORUS

Such wanton spasms of prophecy:
Whence are they engendered?
What drives that pouring out
In molds of melody
Such weird, dejected,   wounded song?
What makes you know this sad prophetic territory?
Its dismal path?

CASSANDRA

I see! I see
Paris make his match:
Death-wedding for his own.
I see Scamander, Father's stream:
Those banks,
O, memory! . . .
I was happy in my rearing.
Now, beside the Cocytus—that crying river—
And on the banks of Acheron in hell
I seem to wail my divinations soon.

CHORUS

What did you say? You make your words too clear;
A babe could comprehend.
Red fangs of pain bite deep—
Your threnody of sorrow . . .
My ponder heart is riven.

CASSANDRA

Weep, weep, weep for the pain of my wasted city.
Weep for my father's holocausts made to save its towers:
   All those slaughtered kine that roamed the meadows.
     The uselessness of it
   To keep my town from suffering what it did.
    And now I too, on fire, crash down.

CHORUS

Oh, how this sentiment pursues everything you've uttered!
    What cacodemon falls on you
And presses out those cries so full of death?
    The end, I can't discover.

CASSANDRA

Ah! But now my oracles shall peep no more
   Like a fresh-wed bride behind her veil.
    Limpid as a clear dawn breeze
    That swells against the rising sun,
    They burst like a wave upon his rays
    A far greater sorrow still.

   No longer shall I speak in riddles.
   And you, hot followers on the trail,
Be witnesses and pace me in the scent
    Of those faraway crimes.

There rises from these halls in single voice
    A perpetual choir,
   A jangled symphony of ill,
    With ill its theme.
   Blood drinkers come in sisterly riot,
    Impassioned in their cups—
     The Erinyes—
Cling to the house and will not be dismissed.
Lurking in the rooms, they hymn their hymn
    To that original lapse,[27]

[27] The murder of Myrtilus: first crime in the long history of the house of Pelops.

And spit in turn their strains of hate
On the man who fouled his brother's bed.[28]

    Did I miss?
      Or hit it, like an archer, straight?
Am I some fortuneteller, babbling lies from door to door?
      Come, swear it:
    I know this house's ancestry—
      Its pedigree of sin.

CHORUS

    What's in an oath?
What's curative in honor sworn?
And yet I am amazed that you,
    Bred beyond the seas,
Speak of a foreign town as if you had been there.

CASSANDRA *and* CHORUS

CA: Apollo, god of prophets, gave me to the office.

CH: What! Was a god in love with you?

CA: I blushed to tell this tale before.

CH: Personal success makes people prim.

CA: But his courtship was a hot sweet-breathing thing.

CH: And put you in the family way, as these things do?

CA: Not that. I promised Loxias but broke my word.

CH: Did you already have the gift of prophecy?

CA: Yes: even then foretelling the disaster of my town.

CH: And Apollo's anger left you quite unscathed?

CA: Since that mistake, no one will believe a thing I say.

CH: Well, to us at least what you say seems credible.

---

[28] Thyestes, who seduced Aërope, wife of Atreus his brother.

CASSANDRA

[Wincing in wild ecstasy]

Oh! The pain! The pain!
Truth comes racking me again.
That overture to prophecy:
It spins me round and turns my head.
There—see them? Over there, above the house:
    Those little ones,
  Like phantoms in a dream.
Don't they have the look of children
    Murdered by their dearest?
    Their hands are crammed with meat,
    Meat of their own flesh:
  Bowels and entrails proffered up
    (What bitter armfuls!),
    For their father's feasting.

Because of this, I say, a vengeance waits:
  In his bed a certain lion [29]
Crouches cowardly, and watches—
    Oh, treachery!—
    For my master's coming . . .
  (*Master*, yes—I am a slave).

And the Lord High Admiral,
  Ravener of Ilium,
Has no idea of what the bitch's tongue has said:
  Its hate, its hidden kiss of death,
  As she licks and fawns and pricks her ears,
  Plotting the very hour and stroke.

Ah! that unleashed female beast to kill a man.
What monster shall I call her? What abomination?

[29] Aegisthus

An "amphisbaena"—each end a sting?
A scylla lurking: rock-witch ruin of sailors?
    A hell-born hag,
Breathing fire and slaughter on those most dear?
    The effrontery of that cry of hers!
    Like a battle rout of triumph
Supposedly for joy at his return.

And whether you believe or not—what matter now?
      It comes what comes.
    And you who stand here will profess,
      Too soon but pitifully:
    "She was too true a prophetess."

CHORUS

Thyestes feasting on his children's flesh,
  That I understood and shuddered at:
A monstrous fact and no fictitious parable.
The rest is only words for me: I'm off my track.

CASSANDRA *and* CHORUS

CA: Agamemnon dead is what you'll see, I say.

CH: Quiet, girl! Don't say it. Trim your tongue.

CA: No doctoring here to dress the truth.

CH: If that be true, there's none; but heaven avert!

CA: You pray! while others prime themselves to slay.

CH: What man in Argos could so plot?

CA: You've missed my meaning utterly.

CH: Have I so? The method and the murderer?

CA: Even though my Greek is good—too good.

CH: The Delphic oracles are Greek, and riddles too.

CASSANDRA

[*In another spasm of possession*]

Oh, fire! what fire! . . . It's on me now.
Apollo, 'Pollo, Light . . . What pain!
She, the two-footed lioness,
Couching, covered, by the wolf
When the royal lion is gone—
She will hack me down: the stricken one.
       Oh, she swears it!
In the poison of the draught she brews,
   Drops of her anger mix for *me*
   As she whets the edge of her sword for *him:*
To pay us back in bloody vengeance for my bringing here.

Away then with these mockeries of myself I wear:
   This wand, this sibylline chaplet at my throat.

                              [*She tears off her insignia
                              and throws them to the ground*]

       Down with you!
   Out and damn you first before I die!

                              [*She tramples on them*]

       There . . . lie still.
   I am equal with you now.
Decorate another wretch's death—not mine.

                              [*She slips out of her dress*]

See! Apollo himself defrocks me from my mantic gear:
   This uniform of his which made me cheap
       (While he looked on)

Before my friends; among my foes:
A most unanimous fool, a tramp,
A quack, a starveling beggarwoman.
      I took it all; and look:
The prophetess undone precisely by the prophet—
      Herded to this dying-place.
The altar stone they slew my father on
            Is now a block
            Ready for me—
For that scarlet stroke of smoking butchery.

Surely we shall not die and the gods be dumb?
One day a young avenger shall arrive,[30]
            A shoot of the stock:
Both matricide and patri-punisher.
Exile, outlaw, ostracized from here,
            He shall come back
      To fit the copingstone of sin
Upon the perfect disenchantment of this house.
            There is an oath in heaven,
            Whose adamantine force—
His father's prostrate body—pulls him home.

Why then should I lament beside this wall?
I who once saw Ilium taken as they took her,
And then her captors reap their just reward in God's
                                          design.

      I shall go, and do, and dare to die.
These gates of death I shall accost and say:
"Let the stroke be true;
   No struggle there ensue,
That in the panting burst when life's blood flows,
These my eyes in easy death shall close."

                        [CASSANDRA *begins to move*
                           toward the palace doors]

30 Clytemnestra's son, Orestes, who in *The Libation Bearers* comes
back to punish his mother.

CHORUS

Most wretched woman and most wise,
 You stretch your time!
 Yet, with your death so known,
How do you step with courage to the altar stone?
 Like a heifer led by heaven.

CASSANDRA *and different* ELDERS

CA: Strangers, where there's no escape,
                     postponement is no profit.

OLD MAN: Yet honor lasts right to the very end.

CA: This day has come, and little should I gain
                                        by flight.

ANOTHER: Oh, you are brave: a most undaunted soul!

CA: Only the lost are paid that compliment.

ANOTHER: And yet there's grace for man to die
                                    heroically.

CA: Oh, my brave father—and your noble sons!

[*She starts back from
the door in horror*]

ANOTHER: What is it now? What terror turns you back?

CA: Foul! Foul!

ANOTHER: What's foul but in your fraught imagining?

CA: The room—it reeks! Drips red with murder.

ANOTHER: Only the animal victims at the hearth.

CA: A breath from an open grave.

ANOTHER: Hardly our costly Syrian incense!

CASSANDRA

So, then I go
To sing the dirge of my own demise
And Agamemnon's too within the palace.
Enough of life! O unknown men, good-bye!
I am no little bird that quivers at a bush's stir.
But when I am dead and when you see
A woman for a woman die,[31]
A man for a man ill-mated lie,[32]
Then remember what I said:
My dying wish—remember it—my prophecy.

CHORUS

Pity you, maiden, for such predestined dying!

CASSANDRA

Once more, one word—but not *my* dirge.
In the sun's last light I ask the sun:
"Let my slayers pay the price of me in blood—
A dying slave; poor easy prey."
So much for human happiness
Whose heady day
A shadow can make fall;
Who in dismay
One wet dash can sponge away:
A picture totally destroyed—
Unkindest cut of all.

[CASSANDRA *walks through the doors into the palace.
The* CHORUS *groups for a song of sadness and vanity*]

[31] Clytemnestra for Cassandra.
[32] Aegisthus for Agamemnon.

CHORUS

O, Success:
Insatiate and sorry thing for man!
Who will bar you from the palaces
        With notices that say:
        "We've had enough, please keep away."?
        Look at him, our king:
Whom Success's gods have given Priam's town,
    Who comes back home to claim divine renown.
        Of what avail, O mortal man?
For now he pays the price of former blood,
        Fulfills a death
By dying for a death those others ran.[33]
        Who would not ask at birth
        Some mute and inconspicuous span?

> [AGAMEMNON's *death groan is*
> *heard from inside the palace*]

AGAMEMNON

O-oh! I am hit . . . mortally hit . . . within.

CHORUS

Listen! Whose shout was that: "mortally hit"?

AGAMEMNON

A-ah!—again! A second time . . . hit.

---

[33] Atreus, Agamemnon's father, killed the children of Thyestes. Agamemnon killed his daughter Iphigenia.

CHORUS

The deed is done. You heard the king cry out.
We must confer at once on measures of security.

> [*The old men huddle together
> in a confused group*]

1ST: I tell you what I think: call for help.
        Have the townsfolk hurry to the palace.

2ND: *I* say break in now.
        Convict them with the crime still dripping from
                                  their sword.

3RD: I'm inclined to think so too. Act quickly.
        This is not a time for dithering.

4TH: A *coup d'état!* It's plain.
        They're out to set up tyranny.

5TH: And here we dawdle while they trample every
                          scruple down. . . .
        Their hands are not asleep.

6TH: I can't think of a plan . . .
        It takes a man of action to conceive a plan.

7TH: I think the same. No amount of talk will raise the
                                    dead.

8TH: But there's foul murder in the house.
        We can't give in to that to save our skins.

9TH: Impossible. Far better die.
        Death is bland compared to tyranny.

10TH: All we've heard is groans.
        Do we predict on that the man is dead?

11TH: No. Before we let our passions fly,
        clear fact from fiction first . . . they're not the
                                    same.

CHORUS

So we're all agreed on this at least:
find out what's happened to the king.

[*The doors are opened and inside they see the bodies
of* AGAMEMNON *and* CASSANDRA *lying not far from each
other. The queen, bloodstained, stands over them*]

CLYTEMNESTRA

I was eloquent before . . . I needed it.
I shall not blush undoing every word.
How else could I play hate on hate
Against the love pretended?
Or fence the mesh of ruin round it
High enough that no one could leap out?
This was a long-premeditated struggle
Come to triumph at last—yes, long overdue.
I stand here where I struck him. The thing is done;
And done in such a way
(I shall not disavow it)
As to make all flight and all defense from doom
Impossible.

   Around him like a net of fish
I swung that smothering looseness—
A fatal opulence of gown.
Then I struck him twice,
And with a double groan
His limbs went loose, he fell.
I was on him with a third—"thanksgiving"—stroke:
To the Zeus[34] of the world below, the keeper of the

                                                      dead.

So he went down,

[34] The third libation at feasts was always to Zeus the Preserver of
Life. Clytemnestra says sarcastically that the god she offered her
grace-stroke to was Hades—Preserver of the Dead.

Life pumping out of him
And gurgling murderous spurts of blood
Which hit me with a black-ensanguined drizzle.
Oh, it freshened me like drops from heaven
When the earth is bright and sprung with budding.

    So stands the case, you Argive elders here.
See joy in it—if joy you can—but I am proud.
And if there's grace in pouring ritual wine upon the
                                     dead,

He's had that sacrament—oh, had it royally!
He filled his family's miseries to the brim.
The cup is his; he's home;
The dregs have drained on him.

CHORUS

You shock us with your brazen tongue:
crowing over him—and he your husband!

CLYTEMNESTRA

    You challenge me like any silly woman.
It does not make me nervous in the least.
You know it.
And whether you decide to praise or blame,
It's all the same.
I say to you:
"This is Agamemnon,
My husband and a corpse:
Work of this right hand of mine—a stalwart workman.
And that is that!"

CHORUS

    What flower of evil, woman,
Blistering from the earth,

Have you partaken of?
Or drawn what drink from the swelling sea
To put you under such a spell of blood and universal
hate?

You cast—you cut him off—and cursed you'll be,
Without a city.

CLYTEMNESTRA

So . . . Now you'd have me banished from my city,
Cursed ringingly and hated publicly?
Before—against him lying there—you never spoke a
thing.

Yet *he's* the man who made a victim
(As if she were a beast,
As if he had no fleecy folds to sacrifice) . . .
Of his own daughter—dear lamb of my womb—
To charm the winds from Thrace.
Why was *he* not hustled from the land,
A filthy scapegoat?
Instead, you turn your eyes on what *I've* done:
Rivet me with judgment.

Well, I'll tell you this:
Threaten me, but know we fight on equal terms.
And when you've thrashed me with your own right hand,
Then you can dictate.
But if God works the opposite,
I mean to teach you
A little modesty—be sure of it—though very late.

CHORUS

High and mighty is it? Swaggering words!
You manslaughter-maddened mind,
With murder written on your face!
Yet a little while and you, stripped of your friends—
Stroke by stroke—

Shall make amends.

CLYTEMNESTRA

Very well, but listen to my sworn vow too:
By the perfect vengeance of my child,
By Ate and the powers of hell
(To whom I sacrificed this man),
I shall never tread the halls of terror
So long as my hearth burns bright
Kindled by Aegisthus, loyal as ever by my side.
He is my shield of courage: no flimsy shield.

Here lies the degrader of this woman:
Petted and fooled by every gilded girl at Troy.
And here *she* lies, his battle booty,
Clairvoyant, concubine,
Faithful fortuneteller, bedder down—
Not unfamiliar, either, to the rub of sailors' boards.
A well rewarded pair. . . .
Yes, here he lies, and here is she:
The swan who warbled out her swansong, his beloved,
Leading such a dainty morsel to my bed.[35]

[*In the lyrical dialogue that follows between the* CHORUS *and* CLYTEMNESTRA, *recriminations and self-justifications mingle with a mutual recognition that fate and horror have, from the beginning, dogged the House of Atreus*]

CHORUS

Strophe 1

Oh for a sickness to carry us away

[35] Ambiguous and ironic: (i) Cassandra brings Agamemnon to his wife's bed—to be murdered. (ii) Agamemnon brings Cassandra to his wife's bed—to be murdered. (iii) Cassandra's arrival with Agamemnon, and their joint despatch, installs Aegisthus officially in Clytemnestra's bed.

Shortly, sweetly, soon,
  (No bed of pain)—
To that abiding sleep which knows no end.
Our most bounteous sentinel lies low.
A woman worked him down with many sorrows:
  A woman took his life away.

Refrain 1

Oh, fatal, infatuate Helen!
Many, so many, by one
At Ilium's walls undone:
Yours the red red crowning
  Of blood perennial
  Indelibly blooming.
For within that time within that house
  There was a hurt built in:
    A master's ruin.

CLYTEMNESTRA

O . . . death, let it go
Nor load yourself so
With anger to fall upon Helen as though
  She were the man-eater: one
  Losing the lives of so many
    Men of the Greeks
And wreaking incurable sorrow.

CHORUS

Antistrophe 1

There is a demon then that pounces
On the palace and the two Tantálidae:
  A tyranny crone-matched and mated,
    Oh, a heart-devourer;

Which like a filthy raven stands,
   Obscenely croaking—
   On a corpse—
   Its song of gloating.

Refrain 1

  Oh, fatal, infatuate Helen!
  Many, so many, by one
  At Ilium's walls undone:
  Yours the red red crowning
    Of blood perennial
    Indelibly blooming.
For within that time within that house
  There was a hurt built in:
    A master's ruin.

CLYTEMNESTRA

  Oh, now you set right your opinion
  In branding that family ogre—
Thrice-gorging with lapping of blood,
  Hankering deep in their flesh.
    The scab is not dry
  And a flowing has freshly begun.

CHORUS

Strophe 2

  You tell of a giant demon
  Haunting the house—and heavy his presence.
Bitter, bitter is the story—Oh!
  Of gluttonous obsession . . . Oh,
  Mercy! Mercy! Zeus almighty
  Overruler, what without your
  Will can happen? What of this
  Is not made in heaven?

Refrain 2

O monarch, my monarch, my tears
    How shall they pay you?
Or tell of my fondness, my feeling
    For *you* in that spider's web,
Panting away in an impious death
Your life in that niggardly bed?
      And your lying
      Hacked down to your dying
By the two-cutting, two-serving tool of a wife?

CLYTEMNESTRA

You protest the work is mine. Why not pretend
    I'm *not* Agamemnon's
Wife, but the ruthless ever-old wicked
Spirit of Atreus, barbarous feaster,
Adopting the semblance of corpse's consort
    To pay him with primest of victims
    The price of babies dead?

CHORUS

Antistrophe 2

    Not guilty—you—of his death?
    Where is there one who will witness for you?
Where? And yet his father's evil genius
    Could indeed be dire abettor:
    Black Havoc wading in a flood
    Of a family's living blood
To the chilly reckoning at last
    Of that gory dishful of children.

Refrain 2

O monarch, my monarch, my tears
　　How shall they pay you?
Or tell of my fondness, my feeling
For *you* in that spider's web,
Panting away in an impious death
　　Your life in that niggardly bed?
　　　　And your lying
　　Hacked down to your dying
By the two-cutting, two-serving tool of a wife.

CLYTEMNESTRA

As to his dying, I think it is this:
　　Hardly a niggardly debt.
Did he not bring (and no one but he)
　　To his house insidious Ate?
Dealing my darling sprung-from-him sapling
(The very-much-wept-for Iphigenia)
Such as he dealt and such as he suffered?
So, neither in Hades let him go boasting.
　　　　His death by the sword
Was the death he had paid for and bought and begun.

CHORUS

Strophe 3

Bewildered, bereft of ready expedient,
　　I ask and I anxiously wonder
Where to escape from a house which is falling.
Cowered I wait while the blood-beating rainstorm
Shivers the dwelling, no longer in drops;
And Destiny whets on another whetstone
　　Vengeance for another disaster.

Refrain 3

Dust of the earth, O dust receive me
Before I should ever have lived to see
My master floored on a silver laver.
Who shall bury him? Who shall mourn him?
You perhaps—you—in a final affront,
As husband-killer shall pour out a wailing;
Cheering his soul with a cheer of no meaning,
With the wish of redeeming your monstrous crime.
And who at the hero's funeral oblation,
          Streaming with tears,
     Shall keen with a genuine sorrow?

CLYTEMNESTRA

This is no business of yours.
          We are the cause
Of his downfall and death. And down in the sepulcher
We shall inter him with no lamentations
From any at home. For Iphigenia,
          His daughter, becomingly
          Greeting her father
     At the swift-flowing ferry of sorrows,[36]
     Shall fling out her arms
     Around him and kiss him.

CHORUS

Antistrophe 3

So rebuke has come to return the rebuke!
     Difficult too to decide:
Looter is looted, killer is killed;

[36] "Ferry of sorrows": Mr. Louis MacNeice's excellent rendering.

Zeus on his throne, the Abider, is biding
By the law that the criminal suffers. Ah, *that*
Is the statute. And who can expel from the house
Seeds of a curse in their blood when the race
    Is welded deep to calamity?

Refrain 3

Dust of the earth, O dust receive me
Before I should ever have lived to see
My master floored on a silver laver.
Who shall bury him? Who shall mourn him?
You perhaps—you—in a final affront,
As husband-killer shall pour out a wailing;
Cheering his soul with a cheer of no meaning,
With the wish of redeeming your monstrous crime.
And who at the hero's funeral oblation,
    Streaming with tears,
    Shall keen with a genuine sorrow?

CLYTEMNESTRA

You've touched on a truth with timely exactness.
I in consequence only too willingly
Swear with the fiend of the house a pact
To let things lie, hard though it be:
May in future he go to worry with death
And self-dissolution some other clan.
Slight be my wealth, but more than enough,
If this series of murderings—fierce, suicidal—
I've swept from these demonized mansions.

[AEGISTHUS, *with an armed
bodyguard, strides in*]

AEGISTHUS

O sweet day of justice ushered in!

At last I can say the gods on high look down
With vengeful eyes upon the crimes of earth,
Now that I see (so sweet to me!)
This creature sprawling out—
Swaddled here in trappings which the Furies spun,
Paying for his father's wicked sleight of hand.

For, Atreus, lord of this land, his father,
Being challenged by Thyestes,
My father and his brother
(I'll tell the story straight),
Drove him from his city and his home.
Then Thyestes, sad, came back,
A suppliant at the hearth,
And found at least this mercy:
That he himself was not to die—
Not splash his death upon his native plot.

But Atreus—godless father of the dead man here—
Outstripping even love in welcome,
Pretended a day of celebration for him:
A great dinner to be carved—
Meat of his own children.
And, sitting apart,
He severed first before he served it
The toes from the rest and the comblike crest of fingers.

My unwitting father
Took those unsuspicious parts and ate—
Meal so poisonous, as you see, for all his race.
Then discovering what he'd done,
He made a cry, reeled back, spewed out the butchered

mess,

Kicked the table over in a curse,
Bellowing out abomination on the House of Pelops:
"Go down so—in ruin—you total race of Pleisthenes."

The consequence you see here:
This man stretched out.
I was the one who sewed this murder up—

So rightly *I*:
Third child of my unhappy father,
Banished with him—
A little thing in baby clothes.

But I am a grown man now.
Vengeance brought me back.
I put the touch of death on him though far away,
Piecing together the final stratagem.
And now,
Death itself I could find sweet,
Seeing him fast at last in Judgment's winding sheet.

CHORUS

Aegisthus, such arrogance in guilt I hate.
You claim you killed this man with full intent;
That all alone you brought his piteous murder off.
I tell you this:
There will not fail to fall upon your head
A rain of stones and curses from the people.

AEGISTHUS

You talk—galley oarsman from the bottom bench!
While *we* are masters on the upper deck.
Good manners are the order, greybeards. . . .
At your age you'll find the schooling hard.
Chains and prison pangs are excellent instructors,
Real doctorers of wisdom—
Even for the old.
Have you eyes and cannot see?
Don't kick against the goad. . . .
You might trip up and dash yourself.

CHORUS

You woman—you!

Lurking back at home
While the men went out to fight;
Then befouling a hero's,
A warrior hero's bed,
And sneaking up to cut him down.

AEGISTHUS

More insults, eh? An extra source of tears.
You have a tongue exactly opposite to Orpheus':
He bewitched the world behind him with his voice;
Your maddening yelps will get you dragged along

                                     yourself,
Quite tamed by force.

CHORUS

Force! So you're to rule in Argos, eh?
The program-plotter of the monarch's end
Who never had the nerve to kill him with his own

                                     right hand!

AEGISTHUS

Of course! The duping was a woman's part,
For *I* was suspect:
A too-established enemy.
With this man's gold however
I'll make a bid to keep you citizens controlled
And clap a heavy collar on the troublesome.
I'll have no barley-pampered trace colt stepping high.
Starvation in a darkened stable
Shall sober him.

CHORUS

Coward!

So you could not kill the king yourself
But had to let a woman do it—
That blot upon her country and her country's gods.
But if Orestes lives,
Is somewhere in the sunlight still,
May fortune speed him home, oh graciously!
To kill the pair of them,—completely kill.

AEGISTHUS

Very well then, be enlightened,
Since your words and acts demand it.[37]

[*He turns toward his men*]

Attention! bodyguard, my comrades.
Come, your work lies close at hand.
'Shun, men! Up and at the ready.
Every man with hand on hilt.

CHORUS

Hand on hilt is ours exactly,
Facing death if need there be.

AEGISTHUS

Dying is it that you speak of?
Luck on it! for die you shall.

[*Draws*]

[CLYTEMNESTRA *flings herself
between the contending groups*]

CLYTEMNESTRA

Not at all, my dearest husband,

[37] The meter used from here to the end of the play—the meter of an "envoi"—is modeled (as are most of the choral lyrics in this *Oresteia*) on Aeschylus's own.

Let us not work further evil:
Even these are far too many,
Far too bitter this a harvest;
Surely cause enough for sorrow.
Let us not be spilling blood.

Hurry, ancients, to your dwellings.
Yield to circumstance and season.
Go before you meet with hurting.
What we did we had to do.
These afflictions—let them stop now;
I am ready—Oh the brutal
Demon's hoof has ground us hard . . .
There—you have a woman's reason:
Fit to hear if any listen.

AEGISTHUS

But insolence like this that blossoms
From their idiot tongues and blurts
Fooleries against me, tempting
Fortune, not restraining any
Insult to their ruler, this . . .

CHORUS

It's hardly like the men of Argos
To cringe beneath a coward's feet.

AEGISTHUS

Just you wait! You'll have a visit
Full of vengeance from me some day.

CHORUS

Not if fortune guides Orestes

Here and brings him home at last.

AEGISTHUS

Idle hope! I know the hunger
Every exile feeds upon.

CHORUS

Go on, glutton, gorge on triumph,
Sewer justice, since you have it.

AEGISTHUS

Do not think you shall not answer
Fully for this foolish insult.

CHORUS

Strut and crow like any rooster
Showing off beside his hen.

CLYTEMNESTRA

Take no notice of their barkings,
Dearest, since they cannot bite.
You and I this house's masters
Now shall order all things right.

THE

LIBATION

BEARERS

for PHILIP WHEELWRIGHT

φιλοκαλοῦμέν τε γὰρ μετ' εὐτελείας
καὶ φιλοσοφοῦμεν ἄνευ μαλακίας

Thucydides

(Yes, we are lovers of the beautiful
but not undisciplined,
intellectuals, but not unmanly)

THE CHARACTERS

ORESTES: son of AGAMEMNON and CLYTEMNESTRA
ELECTRA: his sister
CLYTEMNESTRA: queen of Argos and wife of AEGISTHUS
AEGISTHUS: now king of Argos
CILISSA: ORESTES' old nurse
PYLADES: companion of ORESTES
SERVANT: of AEGISTHUS
CHORUS: of captive Trojan women
ATTENDANTS: of ORESTES, CLYTEMNESTRA, AEGISTHUS

TIME AND SETTING

ORESTES, *returning from exile, recognizes* ELECTRA, *his sister, at the tomb of* AGAMEMNON. *It seems that* CLYTEMNESTRA *has been disturbed by a dream. She has sent out her slaves with* ELECTRA *to offer up libations for the murdered man. After* ORESTES *has made himself known to his sister he conceives a plan of entering the palace with his companion,* PYLADES, *and doing away with his mother and her former paramour, now her husband,* AEGISTHUS.

It is morning; the place is Argos, outside the royal palace, with the tomb of AGAMEMNON *in the background.* ORESTES *and* PYLADES *enter, dressed as travelers.* ORESTES *catches sight of his father's tomb.*

THE

LIBATION

BEARERS

ORESTES

Hermes:
god of my fathers, lord of the dead,
    I invoke you.
Be my champion, be my friend.
I am home again—back on my soil—
and beg my father from this mounded grave
    to hear me and attend.

> [*He advances to the tomb and lays
> a strand of hair upon it*]

One lock, Inachus,[1] for you,
    who fed my manhood;
and here's a second—fed with mourning.
For I was not there, Father,

---

[1] It was the custom for young men to offer a lock of their hair on reaching manhood. The shaving of heads, wholly or in part, was also a token of mourning for the departed.

to break my grief upon your murder
or stretch out my hand towards your bier
and body's passing.

[*As he speaks, a band of captive women in black, the*
CHORUS, *led by* ELECTRA, *emerge from the palace and
make their way towards the tomb. They carry vases and,
in the extravagant manner of the East, beat themselves
and wail*] [2]

But, what do I see?
What solemnities of black
draped upon this throng of women coming?
What matching sorrow?
Some new death to strike the house?
Or is it rather urns of peace
they carry to my father here
to pour out for the dead?

Yes, surely so;
for I think I see my sister there, Electra,
distinguished in her bitter walk of sorrow.
O Zeus,
grant me to avenge my father's fate—
be my ready ally.

Pylades, let us step aside
and let me see
what this processional of women means.

[ORESTES *and* PYLADES *take cover*]

PARODOS
Strophe 1

Straight from the house precipitate
with urns dispatched I come and flying fingers spoiling
new furrows in my face which nails have flared
bright with crimson tearing,

[2] The women who make up the Chorus are ladies of the court
brought back from captured Troy. Expressions of grief which to
the Greeks might seem barbarous were current in Asia. Solon's
later laws forbade them to the Athenians.

while perpetually my heart is fed
  upon perpetual crying.
Ah! loud from my breast is rent that brave
display of vestments, rags, so sorrow-shred,
  and all my smiling shattered.

Antistrophe 1

Keen the bristling horror seen
by a palace dreamer in a dream which deep within
  blasted sleep with hate and broke
  the fabric of the night with shrieking;
  fell like vivid lead upon
the women's walls. The dream-diviners called
    the gods to witness, said:
—the livid underworld was smoldering still
  against the murderers of the dead.

Strophe 2

Such the inhumane humanity that seeks to turn the tide—
    O Earth, kind Earth, my mother!
    She flings me on this errand
    in her hankering anxiety—
      this godless woman.
I fear to stutter out my prayer.
Blood on the ground once spilt, oh what shall ransom?
    Poor desolate hearth.
    Poor house in dereliction.
Sunless abomination glooms
upon the halls of my murdered masters.

Antistrophe 2

The unmatched dignity is gone: invincible, unwon.
    It thrilled the people's hearts and ears
    before. Now fear is felt.[3] Success
alone is god and more than god for man.

---

[3] Perhaps purposely vague. Instead of the old reverence for Agamemnon a slavish fear of Aegisthus holds sway. Yet it is Aegisthus and Clytemnestra who need to fear—if they only knew.

But Justice sits meticulous;
with a tiny tilt unbalances
some from the light, some from the borderland
of semi-dark
where melancholy waits
for the latter day; and some into
the nothingness of night.

Strophe 3

The lusty ground has overdrunk its draft of blood,
dried and clotted with the clamorous gore.
The criminal is racked by Fate.
soaked to his soul in misery to come.

Antistrophe 3

The tampering with the holy covert spot of marriage
is not undone,[4] though all the rivers run
into a single flood to wash
the scarlet hands; and uselessly must run.

Epode

But as for me, the gods have cast a doom
of bondage round my city's walls,[5]
and brought me to a menial's fate where I
must choke my will in galling hate
and force myself to serve
the principalities of right and wrong,
while behind my veil I weep
numb with secret grief
for the frustrate fortunes of my lords.

ELECTRA

Come, you handmaids, sweet orderers of home,
who join me on this suppliant walk,
counsel me in this: what shall I say

4 Aegisthus, as adulterer and murderer.
5 Meaning Troy or Ilium.

as I empty out these urns of empty grief?
What words of grace? What invocation to my father?

Shall I say I carry love—a woman's to a man—
        and mean my mother?
  I have no heart for this, I have no words
  for pouring chrism [6] on my father's tomb.
  Or shall I mouth *this* formula and pray:
"Reward us fittingly for these honored wreaths
  with a gift that—ah!—fully fits the crime"?
    Or in a mute indignity,
      just as my father died,
shall I scatter forth these tributes for the guzzling
                        ground to drink,
    then toss away my urn, step back,
avert my eyes—like someone emptying refuse out?

  Share these counsels with me, friends of mine,
  as in this house we share a common hate.
Do not hide behind your hearts for fear of anyone.
    The fated hour awaits the free
just as it does the foisted subjects of a mighty hand.

Tell me, if you know a better course than this.

            [*The women of the* CHORUS *lay their hands*
                    on AGAMEMNON'S *tomb*]

              CHORUS *and* ELECTRA

CH: By my reverence for your father's tomb, as for a
                         shrine,
     I'll give you what you ask—my closest thoughts.

EL: Speak, from your devotion to my father's grave.

CH: Pronounce blessings as you pour, on persons of
                         good will.

EL: And whom shall I name among my friends for
                         that?

[6] Honey, meal, and oil was the mixture commonly used for funeral libations.

CH: First yourself. Then everyone who hates Aegisthus.

EL: You too, then? Partnered with me in this prayer?

CH: Interpret that as . . . now you know.

EL: Who else should be added to our ranks?

CH: Think of Orestes—though he's far from home.

EL: Him, of course. You advise me well.

CH: After that, the murderers—remember them and . . .

EL: What? What form of words? Instruct my ignorance.

CH: Pray that to them may come some god or man. . . .

EL: You mean, a judge or punisher?

CH: Just say: "One to render death for death."

EL: But in the eyes of the gods is that a pious prayer?

CH: Why not? A stroke for a stroke against your
enemies.

[ELECTRA *advances to the tomb
and begins to pour*]

ELECTRA

Almighty courier of the world above and world below,
        Hermes, lord of the dead,
carry down my prayers for the land of the dark to hear,
    where the spirits guard my father's halls;
        and Earth herself—engenderer of all,
who cherishes and garners back her own fecundity.

And as I pour these lustral waters for the dead,
    I call upon my father and I say:
        Pity me, pity our dear Orestes.
            How shall we rule at home?
                We vagabonds—
            whose mother sold us out,
        and with us bought Aegisthus for her mate:

the very man who lent a hand to cut you down.

I—I am no better than a slave;
Orestes, fugitive from his estate;
    while they—they teem with insolence,
luxuriate in everything your toils have won.
Make Orestes come here by some stroke of luck.
            I'm asking *that*.
        Oh, Father, listen to me, please.
            And as for me,
make me twice as honest as my mother was,
    and twice as dutiful in act.

    That is what I ask, for us.
    For them—our enemies—I beg you, Father,
        let someone to avenge you come.
Redress the balance with a killing for a kill.
    Between my prayer for good and prayer for bad,
    that is what I designate for them.
    As for us, send blessings up above:
one with the gods, the Earth, and all triumphant right.

    These are my prayers poured out with these libations.
        And you can make them flower with grief
        and burst into paeans for the dead.

                [*She begins to pour from her urn*]

CHORUS

Strophe

Break tears for the dead, let drop for the fallen
        lord who is broken,
here where the bulwark of evil and good,
        lavishly washed by libations,
beats back the curse of unprayed-for pollution.
        Listen, oh, listen to me, lord,
    you most holy spirit in darkness.

Antistrophe

Misery, misery, oh. Misery, misery!

      Oh, for a man
strong in his spear to unloosen this house.
      Oh, for the Scythian bow
bent back in the hands of Ares himself
      with javelin a-splinter or hand-
      to-hand clash of the close-hilted sword.

ELECTRA and CHORUS

EL: My father must have now received our tributes
                                through the ground.

[*She is about to come away from the tomb when she
notices the lock of hair*]

      But here is something strange for you to share
                                  with me.

CH: What is it, tell us? In my heart a dread is dancing.

EL: Here on the tomb I see—a clipped curl of hair.

CH: A man's, or some full-waisted girl's?

EL: The clue is obvious. Anyone could guess.

CH: Well then—let youth lead age to knowledge.

EL: None but myself could have cut it.

CH: The ones that ought to offer locks for mourning—
                                  hate.

EL: And yet it is so very like . . .

CH: Whose hair? I must know at once.

EL: . . . so very like my own.

CH: A secret offering from Orestes?

EL: Yes, all too like his tangled curls.

CH: But how could *he* have ventured here?

EL: He could have cut this lock and sent it as a
                              present to his father.

CH: Then, all the more pathetic what you say,
      if he is never to touch his foot upon this land.

ELECTRA

      I feel it too: it breaks upon my heart
and I am stabbed as if a rapier thrust me deep.
      Unslaked from my eyes, undykable its drops,
         a sad winter's flood pours through
            when I see this curl of hair.

What hope have I that someone else, some citizen,
      sports it as his own——this strand?
      Or that the murderess herself has clipped . . .
         oh, no, not she: my mother
            (word so wronged)
      whom such aversion of her children grips.
         And yet, the opposite . . .
could I dare to pronounce it crowned the head of him
      most dear in all the world to me:
            Orestes?
         Ah! Hope flatters me.

      It ought to have a voice:
         kindly, like a messenger's,
and spare me so much turmoil of the soul.
         Oh, this lock!
To spurn or not to spurn it? I wish I knew.
      Severed from the head I hate,
or claiming familyhood with me and partnership in

                                                grief?——

         a jewel set on a grave:
            my father's pride.

CHORUS

      We cry to the gods, they understand
how we are tossed about like sailors in a storm.
      But once in port our tiny seed
      can spring into a mighty trunk.

                              [ELECTRA, *moving away from the tomb,*
                                 has seen something else]

ELECTRA

But look: footprints are here—another sign—
    how like . . . so like, my own.
  Two separate feet have left their marks:
    his own and some companion's.
See how my footsteps match heel and toe with his.
Oh, I am in agony; my wits collapse.

                  [ORESTES *steps forward*]

OR: Pray for the future, its success, in thanking
                  heaven for the present.

EL: Present what? What have the gods fulfilled for *me*?

OR: He whom you prayed for stands before your eyes.

EL: And how do you know for whom I prayed?

OR: Orestes, him—I know. You longed for him.

EL: How exactly have my prayers been answered then?

OR: In me. Look no closer for a friend than me.

EL: Sir, what trick is this you want to catch me with?

OR: Catch myself, then, if I am playing tricks.

EL: You want to laugh at my unhappiness.

OR: At mine as well then, if at yours.

EL: But can it really be Orestes I address?

ORESTES

Do you see me and still not know me:
Though when you looked on this poor lock of mourning
                    hair
  and scrutinized the marks my feet had made,
  then your fancy flew away with you—
    you thought you saw me.

    This strand of hair—

match it against the spot where it was cut
and see how it matches mine . . . a brother's head.
  And see this scarf, your own hands' work,
      the way its weave goes,
    its hunting beasts' design . . .

[ELECTRA *seems ready to collapse with joy*]

Be steady now. Control your ravishment.
    The two of us . . . I know . . .
  for us how bitter have the sweet become.[7]

[ELECTRA *throws herself into* ORESTES' *arms*]

ELECTRA

O dearest treasure of my father's house!
    Sweet seed of our salvation's hope—
      so rained upon by tears:
trust to your strength and you shall win your father's
                          house again.
    Yes—precious sight, you four-parts of my love.
    Who hold the part my father had, bound and declared;
    then my mother's . . . fondness thwarted into hate;
and my poor sister's love in all her barbarous
                          martyrdom; [8]
      and you yourself, my faithful brother:
    the only one to cherish me with pride.
    Might and Right and, third,[9] O sovereign Zeus,
      be on your side.

ORESTES

Zeus, yes, Zeus, take note of what is done.

---

[7] τοὺς φιλτάτους γὰρ οἶδα νῶν ὄντας πικρούς I have translated Aeschylus's
words here in the ironic and more ambiguous sense to which they
lend themselves. Literally: "for us I know how bitter have our most
dear ones become," meaning, of course, their murdered father and
murdering mother.
[8] Her sister, Iphigenia, whom Agamemnon sacrificed at the altar to
get favorable winds for the Greek armada launched against Troy.
[9] Zeus the third, *three* being the mystic and effectual number.

    See the eyrie all deserted,
       the eagle father gone:
death-enfolded in the snaky viper's coils;
the orphaned fledglings gripped by want and famishing,
       too tender still
to lift into the nest their father's load of prey.
    I mean myself. I mean Electra here.
      A fatherless couple in full flight
      from the very home they own.

If you destroy these tender remnants of a father
   who paid you sacrifice and greatly honored you,
where will you find another hand so copious to celebrate?
Destroy the eagle's nest and you can never send again
     a token worth the trust of man.
    This royal root once shriveled up
will never serve your altars on the days of sacrifice.
     Be kind to it and you shall raise
     a mighty from a low estate,
      though now it seems so desolate.

CHORUS

Shh! children, you redeemers of your father's house—
      be silent please.
    Someone might overhear, dear children,
    and with a gossip-loving tongue
    relay it all to those in power:
   those who someday I so want to see
   reeking to their deaths in pitch and flame.

ORESTES

Apollo's great strong oracle shall not forsake me now.
    It told me to accept this challenge,
      loudly cheered me on,
   warmed the gall in me with dire predictions
    if I failed to hound them down—

my father's murderers.

"Give them their turn of death," it said;
"blaze like a bull upon them, to hurt and strip them
bare."

Or else (he said)
I must pay for it with my own sweet soul
amid a swarm of worries:
spells from under the earth, he said,
revelations
of particular malignancy for man.
Leprosies that mount the flesh with acid fangs
and eat its natural pith away;
white mildews sprouting on the mange.

And other onslaughts still, he spoke about,
from the Erinyes,
springing from my father's blood.
For dark is the weapon of the underworld
against the debtor to his fallen family dead:
madness and hallucinations in the night,
eyes straining in the blackness, tortured visions.
They batter him and hustle him from his city-home,
bruise his carcass with a bronze-tipped scourge.

Cut off such a one must be
from share of wine cup and the friendly toast;
barred from the altars by his father's buried ire.
No one receives or lodges with him.
And then one day,
despised, unloved by all,
shriveled in his rottenness and fate—
he dies.

Ought I not to believe such oracles?
Why not,
when even if I disbelieved, the deed must still be done?
Too many cravings coincide in me:
the god's behest,
my father's giant grief,

the loss of my estates,
the scandal of my citizens, those famous ones
  who toppled Troy down with their sterling worth,
now at the beck and call of this brace of women . . .
For Aegisthus is a woman too at heart,
  or must prove it soon if he is not.

CHORUS

By the grace of Zeus, great Destinies—come!
  Press the completion
of this towards the tilting of justice.
For venom of tongue give vent to venom
of tongue in exchange, whilst clamoring Justice
squeezes her dues and shouts for her pay.
For stroke of assassin, assassinate striking
give in exchange. The criminal suffers.
Thus says the wise, the thrice-old saw.

ORESTES

Strophe 1

Father, my father so sad, what word
  or action of mine could I conjure
down from afar like a filtering breeze
  to the purlieus of your chamber,
  a light to match your darkness?
  Nevertheless, my sorrow
given away for the once great house
  of Atreus is glory.

CHORUS

Strophe 2

My son, the fire's [10] yawning

[10] Meaning the funeral pyre, which naturally does not burn the soul.

jaws consume no spirit
of the dead; he vividly blazes
his anger afterwards.
The deceased receives his funeral moan,
the noxious murderer is shown,
    the Dirges antiphone
a hue and a cry on every side
    for parents wronged and father.

ELECTRA

Antistrophe 1

Listen, my father, listen in turn
    to the many tears of my weeping.
Two little children here intone
sorrowful anthems on your tomb;
    beggars and outcasts sheltered,
    welcomed at your sepulcher.
What is the good of it? What without evil?
    How can we out-grapple ruin?

CHORUS

Single Strophe

But, oh, for these the god if he will
can substitute sounds of happier voices,
instead of the threnody over the sepulcher,
ring paeans of triumph through kingly palaces,
pledging home our newly-found friend.

ORESTES

Strophe 3

If only at Ilium,

slashed by some Lycian spear,
Father, you had fallen investing
your palace with auras of glory,
made paths for your children
through lives of commendment,
and mounded beyond the seas a monument
deep with earth, impressively banked,
fit for your family's fame.

CHORUS

Antistrophe 2

Fond to the fond who fell
so beautifully there, the dead.
Under the earth distinct
prince in his majesty.
Minister of the mightiest gods
who in the darkness rule as lords,
he was a king where life awards
the scepter and sway
into the fatal hands of those
whom men obey.

ELECTRA

Antistrophe 3

Not even at Troy
should you fall by the ramparts, my father,
or be with the rest of the spear-ravished crowd
buried by banks of Scamander.
Rather his killers,
killed by their own as he was,
were news of the doom and the death brought in,
learnt from a far-off land by one
totally free from these troubles.

CHORUS

Single Strophe

Ah! daughter, your wish is better than gold,
bigger than bliss north of the wind,
voiced because your wishing is easy.
But wait: the crack of this dual stroke
already resounds to your champions under
the ground and the hands of the rulers are rotten;
accursed are these, and now the advantage
   grows on the side of the children.

ORESTES

Strophe 4

Its impetus strikes on the ear.
Clean as an arrow it darts.
Zeus, Zeus, despatch from below
   too late but death-giving Ate
on the ruthless heart and the reckless hand.
Settle the score . . . even of parents.

CHORUS

Strophe 5

Mine to utter the shout of huzzá
   over the man when he's beaten,
   over the woman when downed.
For why should I try to keep underground
   forever my fluttering fancy,
   when there whips on the prow of my heart
   a biting blast of hatred?

ELECTRA

Antistrophe 4

When will Zeus the Effulgent
bring down his fist with a blow?
Up-at-them! Slam their heads asunder!
    Give back the land a promise.
Out of injustice give back justice.
Listen, Earth, O listen, you princes of darkness.

CHORUS

Single Strophe

Blood is the rule when its drops have spilled
on the ground; a fresh request for blood.
Slaughter screams for the Spirit of Vengeance
to fetch from the first the death it will lay
    on the death it has brought to another.

ORESTES

Strophe 6

Sad, oh, sad is it, Lords of the Underworld.
See it you Curses that seethe from the dead.
See it collapsing, this remnant of Atreus:
    a house in dishonor and lost.
    O Jupiter,[11] where shall we turn?

CHORUS

Antistrophe 5

The strings of my heart are humming with fear

---

[11] I usually use the Greek names for the gods, but do not consider
it an anachronism *in English* to use the Latin form.

again, at the sound of this piteous prayer.
   Once I was full of despair,
and the word that I heard was gloom within.
    But hope again comes,
lifts me up with a new-found strength,
    puts away sorrow and shines
      beautifully beside me.

ELECTRA

Antistrophe 6

And what should we speak of, what more touching
than that which we suffered from those who bore us?
Assuage if you can, but here's no soothing.
For *we* like the wolf are raw
    with the savage heart of our mother.

CHORUS

Strophe 7

I drummed an Arian dirge on my breast
   like a Cissian woman weeping.
Pounded importunate, crowded convulsions, you could
                 have seen it:
   flailing my arms, unbending and beating
   upwards and downwards upon my poor head
    hammered with blows that resounded.

ELECTRA

Strophe 8

   Oh, the brutal shame!
Merciless mother! barbarous march to burial!
   no subjects for a king;

no sorrows draped.
You had the heart to bury him unmourned.

ORESTES

Strophe 9

Yes, shout his outrage out,
but she'll undo that outrage of my father's:
by the help of the immortals,
by my own hands' work,
oh, by my life laid down to ravish hers.

CHORUS

Antistrophe 6

And he was mangled[12]—if you must know.
As she maimed, so she buried him;
keen to consummate a violence
more than your young life could bear:
a father mutilated—listen to it.

ELECTRA

Antistrophe 7

You speak of my father's end: they held me off,
debased, made nothing of me,
kenneled me up like some vicious bitch within.
The crowded spasms of my teardrops came,
fell secret, readier than laughter.
Engrave it on your hearts what you have heard.

[12] The word used is μασχαλίζω: to dismember. The limbs of the murdered person were cut off and dangled under the armpits. This was
done in symbol and hope that now he was disabled and powerless to
take vengeance.

CHORUS

Antistrophe 8

Sink it deep, this tale,
into your ears, through to your soul's still fundament.
This is the way things are.
This is the way your zeal must go
to learn the reaches of a rage undampable.

ORESTES, ELECTRA, CHORUS

Strophe 10

OR: Father, I beg you to be on the side of your own.

EL: And with his weepings *I* shall blend my voice.

CH: This whole company roars out acclaim.
          Rise into the day and hear.
             Oh, hurry to our side!

Antistrophe 10

OR: Join War with War and Right against Right.

EL: But heaven decide the right with the right.

CH: A trembling creeps on me as I hear you pray.
          Destiny's too long delayed,
             but it comes, it comes to those who prayed.

CHORUS

Strophe 11

A dismal pedigree

of inbred pain and jangled fate
   dripping with its wound!
A sad and plaintive heaviness!
Oh, calamity unstaunchable!

Antistrophe 11

   In this house a cure—
  not from others or without
   but savage on itself—
  can staunch this curse with gore.
Such is the song we sing to the gods below.

Single Strophe

Hear us you blessed ones under the ground.
Despatch this prayer, and graciously
cheer on your children to victory.

ORESTES

My father, who succumbed to death no kingly way,
grant my prayer and over your palace give me sway.

ELECTRA

And I too, Father, need from you a grace:
to eradicate Aegisthus, then escape.

ORESTES

So shall the customary and consecrated funeral feasts be
                                    yours.
  Otherwise, your presence goes unbanqueted;
   unportioned with burnt-offered glory

reeking to the earth its relish.

ELECTRA

And I shall pour rich dowries out for you
adorned from my father's home—my wedding feast.
First of the first this tomb shall have my homage.

OR: Great Earth, set my father free above to see the fight.

EL: Great Persephassa, grant us more: a wonderful
                                          success.

OR: Remember the bath, my father, which fobbed you
                                       of your life.

EL: Remember the clever net in which they tangled you.

OR: A trapped animal, Father, in fetters no
                               bronzesmith made.

EL: Ignominiously enveloped by shrewd chicanery.

OR: Does this not sting you into action, Father?

EL: Does that dearest head of yours not rouse itself
                                      erect?

ORESTES

Either impel us in the right which fights for friends
or clinch them in the clinch they caught you in,
if from defeat you'd really snatch a win.

ELECTRA

My father, listen to this last appeal,
look at the fledglings huddled at your tomb.
Be tender to your own: this girl, this boy.
The seed of Pelops do not wipe away;

So, though you died, you never yet were dead.
For children are the saving voices of a dead man's fame.
     Like buoyant corks they float the net
      and in the deep bear up the flaxen lines.
        Please hear us, then.
     It is for *you* these supplications pour.
     You save yourself in honoring our cry.

CHORUS

A cry you've understandably made long:
due amends to his tomb and unlamented lot.
     The rest is action; since you're set on that.
     To work, at once. Put Fortune to the test.

ORESTES

     So be it!
Yet I must ask—and not outside my course—
how comes it that she sent libations out?
     What motive made her, all too late,
     care for a sin she cannot cure?
It is a wretched tribute to the unconscious dead.
     For should one shower out all he has, to pay
     for one man's drop of blood—they say—
     it is a sorry effort still. . . .
Satisfy my question if you know.

CHORUS

My son, I know, for I was there.
     It was her dreams.
Shaken by the flitting terrors of the dark,
     this godless woman sent these offerings out.

OR: Did you hear the dream? Could you repeat it
                      right?

CH: She fancied she gave a serpent birth. That's what
she said.

OR: What was the outcome? How does it go on?

CH: She tucked it up in baby clothes as if it were a child
and when the little horror wanted food,[13]
in her dream she offered it her breast.

OR: How did it not gash her nipple, such a ghastly
thing?

CH: It did. Clots of blood it sucked in with the milk.

OR: No empty dream. This vision means a man.

CHORUS

Shrieking and appalled she woke from her sleep
as the unlit lamps flared up—throughout the palace—
to cheer the queen.
And then she sent these funeral offerings to be
poured,
with hopes they'd make an instantaneous cure.

ORESTES

By the earth, and by my father's tomb,
I pray this dream comes true in *me*.
Yes, I think it tallies all along.
If this snake emerges from the place where I came from,
was snuggled in my baby clothes;
if it mouthed the breast that suckled me,
blent the sweet milk with clotted blood,
and if she shouted out with pain and shock—
then this hideous freak she nursed
means she surely dies: dies viciously.

---

[13] I agree with Dindorf, Buckley, and others in giving this line
to the Chorus.

I turn snake to murder her.
That is what this dream forebodes.

CHORUS

I accept your reading of the portent.
        I hope it happens so.
Give your friends their parts to play,
    explaining what to do or leave undone.

ORESTES

        My plan is simple.
Electra here must go inside;
keep our plans well hidden: *that* I emphasize
    if those who tricked nobility to death
are to be tricked themselves and die in the selfsame snare,
    as Loxias predicted, Lord Apollo,
    who never made a false prediction yet.

Disguised as a traveler, complete with all my gear,
    I with Pylades—whom here you see—
        shall approach the outer gates:
    a traveler with a family friend.
We shall speak Parnassian dialect, both of us,
    and imitate the Phocian accent.
Should no porter at the door smile at us and let us in
    (since the house is quite possessed by evil),
            we shall linger there
in the kind of way that makes a passer-by
    express his odd surmise and say:
"So Aegisthus keeps his caller out—
    or is he at home and doesn't know?"

    But once I cross the courtyard gates
and find that man upon my father's throne,
    and once he meets me face to face,
    lifts his eyes, looks down again,

then—know for sure—
before he can say: "The stranger—where is he from?"
I'll flash my sword through him and lay him dead.
Then that Erinys who's never short of blood
will get neat gore to drink for her third carouse.

Now you, Electra, keep a good lookout inside the house
    so that all our plans will coalesce.
You other women, I suggest, keep a careful tongue.
Let circumstances guide your silence and your speech.
    Pylades[14] I ask to superintend the rest:
my organizing second in this saber-lunging test.

[ELECTRA *enters the palace.* ORESTES *and* PYLADES *retire to disguise themselves*]

CHORUS

Strophe 1—First Stasimon

How many terrors the world
produces of mischief and wonder.
The crotches of the sea-deeps
swarm with menace and monsters.
And high in the air swing near
    the shooting torches.
Creatures that fly, and crawlers;
tell of them all and the gusty
    rage of whirlwinds.

But who can tell the flagrant
self-conceit of mortals?
The barefaced will of women
hardened in their passion
mated to man's doomsday,
    whilst lovelorn love
in couplement and union

14 The Greek does not actually say "Pylades," but "him," which some
    editors refer to Apollo whose statue is standing near by.

overpowers the female
     beast and human.

Strophe 2

If any there be with thoughts not flippant,
     let him learn this:
   the callousness and guile
used by that son-slaying woman Althea
   when she thought of the firebrand;
set ablaze the brand of her son blood-red—
brand of his life from the moment he cried
     out from the womb of his mother;
     spanning its life with his,
     on to his foredoomed day.

Antistrophe 2

There's another in legend we're bound to abhor,
     a sanguinary maiden,
        Scylla the traitoress:
who caused the death of her dearest father
     (seduced by a Cretan necklace
fashioned in gold, a present from Minos),
filching the im· ortal hair from Nisus
(breathing away in guileless slumber),
     heart of a dog that she had.
     So Hermes came to take her.

Strophe 3

And since I am telling of evils that harrow,
it is timely to speak of that unloved marriage
     haunting a house; and a woman—
secretive wife who plotted the life
     of a man and a hero in armor;
of a man who could make his enemies cower.

Give me the hearth of a house which is cold
to assertive conceit; and a meekness of woman.

Antistrophe 3

But the Lemnian horror presides in legend:
prime, regrettable, odious, painful.
    The Lemnian horror became
the pattern and image of every calamity:
    the disgrace of the heaven-abhorred
stroke which removed a tribeful of men.
No one respects what the gods find disgusting. . . .
Is any *one* of these tales unfair?

Strophe 4

    Because of the Right the sword
is keen-tipped, ready to strike right through
the lungs. For surely it is not fit
for every sovereign credit of Zeus
to be flouted and trampled under foot.

Antistrophe 4

    The anvil of Justice is firm.
Destiny forges and hammers her steel
already. The famous and pondering Fury
contributes a son to the house at last
to pay for murders gone stale, and pollution.

[ORESTES *and* PYLADES *come in
and approach the palace*]

ORESTES

    Boy—there—boy!
Don't you hear me pounding on the door outside?

Is anybody in there, boy? I repeat, boy—anyone at
                                                home?
This is my third attempt to summon someone from the
                                                house.
    Is Aegisthus given to hospitality *at all*?

SERVANT

[*opening*]

    Yes, I hear you, sir.
        A visitor from where—where from?

ORESTES

Go and tell the masters of the house I'm here to see
                                                them—
        with news.
            Be quick about it.
            Night's dark chariot advances.
    It is the hour when voyagers must drop their anchors
        In some haven kind to strangers.
        Can the lady of the house come out?
            Or better still the master?
    Then no delicate politeness will cloud our talk.
Men to men are clear and speak straightforwardly.

[CLYTEMNESTRA *appears at the door*]

CLYTEMNESTRA

    Friends, you have only to declare your needs.
        A house like ours has everything:
    hot baths, beds to charm away fatigue,
            and eyes laid out to please.
    But if it's something else, some business to transact,
    that's man's affair and we'll get in touch with them.

ORESTES

[*stepping forward*]

Madam, I am a visitor from Daulia in Phocia.
I was traveling to Argos, carrying my pack, on business
                                            of my own,

    when just as I set out I met a man
      (unknown to me as I to him)
who asked me my way and volunteered directions.
He was called—as I found out in conversation—
Strophius the Phocian. And he said:
"Since, my friend, you're going to Argos anyway,
   here's a very special message for the parents of Orestes:
tell them he is dead. . . . You won't forget it, please.
Whether his friends will want to bring him home
or bury him in the land he settled in—a permanent
                                            sojourner—

    bring their decision back to me.
    His ashes meanwhile are enclosed within the walls of a
                                            bronze urn;

    and he's a well-wept man."

    That is what I heard, and tell you.
I do not know if by chance I speak to someone this
                                            concerns,

    but his father ought to know about it.

CLYTEMNESTRA

    Ruin absolute!
    Your words dismantle us.
This house's curse—there is no hold against it.
How wide the vision ranges: that panoramic aim.
Everything we laid away brought down,
   hit to the heart from far.
You strip me, hew me utterly, of friends.
And now, Orestes; so carefully kept clear;
his foot made safe against the deadly swamp;

fair hope and antidote of all this dynasty's debauch—
    now do you write it down as quite deserting us?

ORESTES

I—I could have wished with hosts so bounteous
to have been introduced and welcomed as a herald of
                                some happiness.
    For what is more felicitous
than the exchange between entertainer and entertained?
But it seemed to me a breech of sacred duty
    not to do this obligation for my friends,
pledged as I am by promise and by hospitality.

CLYTEMNESTRA

No, your reception shall *not* fall short of your deserts,
    nor you be any less this house's friend.
    Someone would have brought the news in any case. . . .
And now it is time for travelers after a long day on the
                                road
        to have some comfort.

[*Turns to* SERVANT]

Conduct this gentleman with his retinue [15] and friend
    to our guest wing for the men.
And there they can enjoy the proper comforts of the
                                house.
    Carry it out with care—*you* are responsible.
Meanwhile we shall get in touch with the masters here,
and with our numerous friends deliberate our loss.

[*All leave except the* CHORUS]

CHORUS

    Come, dear handmaids of the house,

[15] Although no mention has been made of anyone else but
Pylades, it is taken for granted that Orestes—a freeborn Greek and
a royal personage—would be attended by two or more slaves.

when shall our lips
discover their strength and fight for Orestes?
You holiest Earth and holy barrow
resting your eminence high on the body
    of the king of the fleets and a monarch:
Now you must listen, *now* you must help us.
Now is the time when Credence by cunning
enters with Hermes into the underworld,
into the night and into the lists
    to marshal that murderous sword.

He seems to have touched on pain, our stranger-man,
for look, I see Orestes' old nurse coming, and in tears.
    Where are you going, Cilissa,[16] past the palace gates
    with this forced companionship of sorrow?

[CILISSA *enters distraught*]

CILISSA

That domineering woman wants Aegisthus called at once
to meet those strangers and find out exactly man to man
what the news is that has just come in. And, oh, before
                                        the servants
her sham gloom eyes were really laughing—laughing
                                        for what has turned
so beautifully for her but so absolutely horrifying for
                                        this house, which
none can doubt at all after listening to these gentlemen;
and when it comes to him it's going to cheer his spirits,
                                        that it will,
when he hears the story. Oh, I'm so unhappy!

You don't know how the past, with all that mix-up of
                                        disasters,
impossible ones, hitting at this poor house of Atreus,
has plucked my living heart from me, but this—
I've never had a blow like this before.

16 Slaves were often called by the name of the country or town they
  came from. Cilissa was a region in Asia Minor.

I put a brave face on all those other setbacks, but—
my darling Orestes whom I wore my soul out for . . .
had him from his mother, nursed him the moment he was
                                                          born—
oh, up all night with his crying, so loud and so demanding.
And the little nuisances put up with . . .
A baby's got no sense at all; just like an animal:
it has to be nursed—of course it must!—and humored
                                                          too.
It can't say a word, wee mite—all wrapped up in baby
                                                          clothes—
whether it's hungry or thirsty or wants to wet . . .
children's little new insides just work the way they want.
But *I* could tell all right; though many's the time I've
                                                          missed
(I should *think* so!) and had to wash the baby's linen out
and turn myself into nurse and washerwoman all in one.
It was a double job I got when I took Orestes from his
                                                          father. . . .
And now I'm told he's dead. And I am so unhappy, and
I'm on my way to fetch the very man
who *was* this family's ruin. Oh, he'll be glad enough to
                                                          hear of it.

                    CHORUS *and* CILISSA

CH: And how did she tell him to come? Prepared?

CI: Prepared? What? Please repeat your question for
                                                          me.

CH: I mean, with guards? Or altogether unattended?

CI: She said: "Bring your bodyguard, and armed."

CH: No: don't tell our hated master that.
            Just tell him to bring himself,
                cheerfully and quickly.
            He mustn't be alarmed. . . . Ha! the messenger
                straightening out the message!

CI: But *you* don't think this news is happy, do you?

CH: It all depends. If Zeus will change a bad wind into
                                                    good . . .

CI: But how? With all our hopes—Orestes—gone?

CH: Not quite. Only a poor prophet would see it so.

CI: What are you saying? Do you know a different
                                                    story?

CH: Go. Just go and give your message as she told you.
      The gods provide for what they will provide.

CI: I shall go then, and do things as you say.
      May all be for the best in Providence's way.

[CILISSA *hurries out*]

CHORUS

Strophe 1—Second Stasimon

Now to my prayer come Zeus the Father,
sire of the gods on high Olympus.
Lavish on those who long to see it
a reign of goodness, rooted good.
   Every syllable's truth.
   Great Jupiter, guard it.

Single Strophe

Yes, set him up face to face
   with his enemies in the house.
Let him loom large, O Zeus,
   and merrily he'll requite
   double and triple in pay.

Antistrophe 1

Think of the yearling whose father you loved
traced and dragging a wagon of sorrows.
Set him bounds for his running, we want to see

him prancing the course steady in stride,
    pacing home at a rhythm,
    champion over the field.

Strophe 2

And you, you gods of the hearth,
cushioned in comforts deep in the home:
    spirits of sympathy—hear.
Finish the things that were done before.
Wash away blood with blood that's fresh.
    Make tottering murder cease
    spawning through the halls.

Single Strophe

And you who so beautifully dwell
    in the cleft of the mighty shrine,[17]
let the hero's house look up with joy:
    lit by the radiant light,
    smiling at the sight
of liberty through the parted gloom.

Antistrophe 2

May Mercury, son of Maia,
send the support for the right he ought,
    since nobody better than he
    can waft a fair wind when he will.
All that lies secret *he* can make plain.
    He utters his mystic word;
mantles our eyes with the darkness of night;
    keeps mystery there in the day.

Strophe 3

So, at last we shall sing

---

[17] Apollo's inner sanctuary at Delphi was a narrow vault or cave
in which stood a tripod. Over the tripod was a slab on which the
Pythoness sat.

for the loosening of this house
with the breeze of a maiden's voice:
(no wraith-drawn whine of lament)—
the song of, "The ship comes home." The gain
is mine, is mine, it gathers until
   evil retreats from my friends.

Single Strophe

Be brave when your part in the business comes.
      With a loud cheer of "Father"
      as *she* cries: "My son!"
      despatch this salutary doom.

Antistrophe 3

With Perseus in your mind,
lift up your hearts with him.
For your friends beneath the earth,
for your friends above, prefer
a brutal rage to joy. Perform
the scarlet stroke; erase the cause
   of criminal and crime.

[AEGISTHUS *enters*]

AEGISTHUS

I have been asked to come here: called by messenger.
      It is hardly a pleasant rumor that I hear,
            Orestes' death,
            started by some people coming in.
            Such a load
added to a house already sore and ulcerous with
                                             slaughter
      would make it ooze and wince.
   Yet how am I to tell if this is living truth
      and not just frightened female gossip
            which flares up in the air
            then fades away?

Can you tell of any sense in this, and clear my mind?

CHORUS

We heard indeed.
But go inside and find out from the visitors.
No report is quite as good as what a person makes
himself.

AEGISTHUS

Then I wish to see the messenger and pin him down.
Was he near the dead man when he died?
Or is he only telling what he heard by common rumor?
You cannot cheat a mind that's open-eyed.

[*He goes into the palace*]

CHORUS

Zeus, Zeus—how shall I frame or begin
a prayer overwhelmingly hopeful, importunate,
wild with desire?
it beggars all praying to suit it. For now
either the man-murdering, blood-tipped
blades are about to put out forever
Agamemnon's line, or else a light
blazing for liberty's sake
is ready to strike—Orestes to master
the rule and domain of his city and also
the joy and wealth of his father's.
Such is the struggle Orestes the godlike
alone against two is pitted to wrestle.
Oh, may it turn into triumph.

[AEGISTHUS'*s death-cry is heard within*]

Aha! Aha!

CHORUS

So it works—ha ha!
But how does it work? How does it stand in the palace?
Hold yourselves back till the business is done.
We must not seem to be part of this horror.
The battle perhaps is over and won.

[*The* CHORUS *shelters behind the tomb. A* SERVANT
rushes out of the palace]

SERVANT

Awful! Terrible! Complete!
My master hit.
Yell it out three times: oh, awful! Aegisthus is no more.

[*He runs to the gate of the women's court*]

Open up at once.
Slide the bolts back to the women's wing;
it takes a lusty arm. . . .
Why try to help the one that's down—no good in that!
Hullo there! Hullo!
Am I shouting to the useless deaf
or people hopelessly asleep?
Where is Clytemnestra? What is she doing?
Her own neck is on the razor's edge—
oh, if I'm right—
ready to feel it fall . . .
the stroke and sentence.

[CLYTEMNESTRA, *unattended, hurries in*]

CLYTEMNESTRA

What is this? The meaning of this shouting through the
house?

SERVANT

The dead, I tell you—now—the living—kill.[18]

CLYTEMNESTRA

O my soul! His riddle is clear.
As we slew, so are we caught for slaying.
Give me an ax—quick—an ax to fell a man.
We shall see who masters or is mastered now.
For I have come to that: the crisis of this curse.

[*The* SERVANT *throws open the inner doors, to reveal
the body of* AEGISTHUS, *with* ORESTES, *sword drawn,
standing over it.* PYLADES *is at hand*]

ORESTES, CLYTEMNESTRA, PYLADES

OR: You're the one I'm looking for. *This* wretch has had
                                                    enough.

CL: Oh, no! Aegisthus dead? . . . *you* my strong
                                                    beloved!

OR: You love that man? Then in the same grave with
                                              him you'll lie:
        faithful unto death and ever afterwards.

CL: Wait, son, wait. My baby, soften
            towards this bosom where so many times
            you went to sleep, with little gums
            fumbling at the milk which sweetly made you
                                                    grow.

OR: Pylades, what shall I do? Weaken and not kill my
                                                    mother?

PY: Then what becomes of the oracles Apollo spoke,
            those oracles at Pythia,

---

[18] I have kept the gruesome ambiguity of the Greek: τὸν ζῶντα καίνειν
τοὺς τεθνηκότας λέγω "the dead are killing the living man," or "the
living are killing the dead man."

and all our solemn oaths?
Make the world your enemy but not the gods.

OR: Your word wins. It is good advice.

[*Turns on his mother*]

Come here. I'll drop you slaughtered by his side.
You thought him finer than my father while he
lived.
Go then: sleep with him in death.
You love this man and hate the one you ought to
love.

CL: I reared you up from babyhood. Oh, let me then
grow old with you.

OR: What! Slay my father—then come sharing homes
with me?

CL: Fate, my son, is half to blame for that.

OR: Then Fate arranges for your dying now.

CL: Son, does a parent's curse mean nothing to you?

OR: Not a thing. You gave me birth, then flung me out
—to misery.

CL: No, no—into a friend's house. Is that to fling?

OR: Shamefully sold. A freeborn father's son.

CL: Oh? Then where is the price I got for you?

OR: *That*, in public, I should blush to say.

CL: Then blush as well for those senseless things your
father did.

OR: Do not taunt him. *You* sat at home. *He* toiled.

CL: Child, a woman suffers when a husband goes.

OR: Oh yes, his pain supports them as they sit at home.

CL: Your heart, it seems, my son, is set on murdering a
mother.

OR: You are the one, not I, who does the murdering.

CL: Watch, then, for a mother's curse: it will hound you
                                                        down.

OR: Or a father's if I let this go.

CL: Am I crying my life away upon a tomb?

OR: Yes. My father's fate is beckoning yours.

CL: So *you* are the snake I bore and gave my breast to?

ORESTES

Yes. Your nightmare saw things straight.
You killed a man you never should,
now suffer what you never would.

[ORESTES *forces his mother into the
palace, followed by* PYLADES]

CHORUS

Even in them it hurts me to the core:
        this double tragedy.
But Orestes at last masterfully rides
        high in that tide of blood.
            He is our choice:
this house's eye must not go out.

Strophe 1—Third Stasimon

It came in the end, Justice, to Priam's—
        justifiably hard—
it came as well to Agamemnon's house.
Leapt with two lions, left two ruins.
            Plunged to the hilt
            by the Pythian pilgrim,[19]
Cheered from above; incited *on*.

---

[19] I.e., Orestes, who had been consulting the oracle at Delphi.

Refrain

Shout your hurrahs for our prince's house,
safe from the wreck or its wealth worn away
    by that purulent pair,
      or on to an end forlorn.

Antistrophe 1

It comes what has come, the covert attack,
    the foxy maneuver, revenge.
Her hand in the fray was stolidly there—
the daughter of Jupiter (Justice, we call her,
    perfectly scoring her name),
      fanning her wind
of fury and death on those she abhors.

Refrain

Shout your hurrahs for our prince's house,
safe from the wreck of its wealth worn away
    by that purulent pair,
      or on to a pitiful finish.

Strophe 2

All of which Loxias, lordly possessor
of that reft in the ground so great on Parnassus,
boldly arranged in a trick without tricking,
and set on the sin that had lasted.
The word of the Lord has a might of its own
strong enough somehow never to serve
the way of the wicked. We worship so rightly
    the puissance of heaven.

Refrain

Look at the light that has come.
The pinch of the bridle has gone.

Lift up your heads, ye halls: too long
   scattered over the ground.

Antistrophe 2

Presently Time the perfecter will pass
over and through the gates of the palace
when all this pollution is driven away
   and holy ablutions have purged
the haunting. And throws of the dice shall fall
full of good luck, with faces that smile
up at the lodgers who once again come
      to live in the palace.

Refrain

Look at the light that has come.
The pinch of the bridle has gone.
Lift up your heads, ye halls: too long
   scattered over the ground.

[*The doors of the palace open and disclose* ORESTES *standing over the bodies of* CLYTEMNESTRA *and* AEGISTHUS. *With him are* PYLADES *and* ATTENDANTS. *They display the robe in which* AGAMEMNON *was murdered*]

ORESTES

   Gaze on them:
the double-headed tyranny of our land;
palace pillagers, my father's murderers. . . .
Once so full of pride as they sat their thrones:
   Still so full of love—
   to judge by what befell.
   Their mutual vows hold fast.
They leagued themselves in pact with death
   against my martyred father;
      in league to die.
Their oath they perfectly fulfilled.

[*He points to the robe*]

Look again, if you would peep your mind at ruin:
the device, the noose, the manacles—oh, my poor
father!—
    his hands, his feet, the fettering.
      Open it out.
      Stand in a circle around it.
      Display—a shroud for a man.
So shall a certain father see—no, not mine
    but the wide all-seeing sun—
    my mother's filthy handiwork.
And he shall stand as witness for me, one day when I am
tried.

I pushed her to this death with right: my mother.
    Aegisthus' end I leave aside:
    wages of adultery which rule prescribes.
    But this woman—this plotter who upset her man,
    by whom she carried children underneath her zone,
    once joyous weight and now proved bitter load—
    what does she seem to you?
    Some deadly moray, some adder-born,
whose touch would shrivel long before her bite
by very force of poison in the will.

[*He takes up the robe*]

    How can I address this thing,
choosing even syllables of gold?
      A wild beast's trap?
Curtain for a body, bier, or bath?
      A winding sheet?
Certainly a net—call it that.
A snare, a cloak-of-folds to trip a man:
exactly what some highwayman might get himself
to trick his travelers, ply his robber's trade.
How many he could catch and kill with this,
    and warm his murderous joy.

Live with a wife like that? Never such a one.

Annihilate me sooner, and leave no living son.

CHORUS

Weep, weep, weep for the crime.
Death was cruel; death dispatched you.
        Oh! Oh!
Pain in the bud for the life left behind.

ORESTES

Did she do it or did she not?
        Here is the witness:
a mantle tipped with the spill of Aegisthus' sword.
Blood and the stale stain of time here blend
        to hurt its many purfled hues.
Now am I weeping.[20] Now I moan, so near him;
invoking this—this patricidal web of folds.
        I feel the pain of it:
offense and punishment . . . oh, race entire.
There is no zest in victory so maculate.

CHORUS

What human soul can pass through life
untouched by suffering to the end?
        Oh, no, there's none.
One sorrow for today, another for tomorrow, comes.

ORESTES

[*With sudden wildness*]

Then *you* know best and I am blind to where it ends.
    Like a charioteer plunging off the course
    I cannot rein my bolting spirits in.
    Next to my heart a bursting terror waits

---

[20] The Greek is: νῦν αὐτὸν αἰνῶ. I cannot understand why translators
and commentators persist in choosing αἰνέω (to praise) instead of αἰνῶ
(to moisten with tears).
    The point is that the sadness and horror of *both* murders (and *all*
murder) is becoming associated in the minds of Orestes and the
Chorus. The first step in Orestes' "Madness."

to mewl and prance.
But, still in my senses, I assert,
     I tell you, friends:
I killed my mother and was justified,
raddled as she was with my father's murdering.
     And the spell that made me dare so much
     I owe to Loxias the Prophet,
          whose oracle declared
that if I did this thing I was beyond the reach of blame,
          but if I slighted it,
no arrow from a bow could touch such peaks of agony.

[*He puts on the suppliant's wreaths of wool and takes
an olive branch in his hand*]

     See me now as I walk,
     arrayed in olive branch and wreathed,
     towards that center-stone and shrine
          where Loxias treads;
     that fabled fire—everlasting bright;
     fleeing from this bloodshed of my own.
There is no other sanctuary, Apollo said, where I must
                                        turn.

     Be witnesses to me in time to come,
     all you Argives, how these miseries came.
And now an exile from this land, a vagabond,
     this fame of mine—in life and death—I leave behind.

CHORUS

     No, you did well.
You must not load your lips with such defeat;
     abuse your tongue with failure.
     You liberated all the state of Argos:
In one fine stroke lopped off two dragons' heads.

[*The* FURIES, *visible only to* ORESTES, *are seen rising
in the background*]

ORESTES

No! Too ghastly! No!
Women of the house, see them—there.
Like Gorgons draped in black,
teeming with their serpents knotted.
I cannot stay here.

CHORUS

Orestes, most precious father's son,
what fancies make you reel?
Grip yourself and do not be afraid. For you have won.

ORESTES

These are no fancies, these agonies of mine.
As clear as day I see them: my mother's foaming pack.

CHORUS

New blood still reeking from your hands:
this is what convulses, smites you to the brain.

ORESTES

Lord Apollo! . . . Now they crowd on me,
distilling blood-drops from their eyes, hideously.

CHORUS

Apollo, yes! A signal purge for you.
His touch can loose you from these throes.

ORESTES

You do not see them. But *I* see them.
I am driven, driven—I cannot stay.

[He rushes out]

CHORUS

Then blessings go with you. And sweeter care
God guard you with in all your life's affair.

[*The* CHORUS *begins to move away, chanting*]

Envoi

So has the third of these tempests raged
        all through the kingly halls;
blown itself past and into seed.
First to come was that grisly feast
        of man-eaten children.
Next to break was a king's catastrophe:
stabbed in a bath he went to his end,
        war-lord of Hellas.
Now shall I say the third has come:
        savior or is it
            nemesis?

Oh, when shall it finish, when shall it sate—
lie down to sleep—this fury-bound hate?

THE

EUMENIDES

for RICHARD HAYES

on whose shoulders, I believe,
falls the luminous mantle of Stark Young

THE CHARACTERS

THE PYTHIA:	priestess of APOLLO
APOLLO:	patron of the Delphic shrine
ORESTES:	son and murderer of CLYTEMNESTRA
HERMES (silent):	messenger of the gods
GHOST OF CLYTEMNESTRA:	late queen of Argos
CHORUS OF EUMENIDES:	the ERINYES or FURIES
PALLAS ATHENA:	patron goddess of Athens
SECOND CHORUS:	women of Athens

OFFICIALS OF THE COURT

HERALD } all silent parts

CITIZENS OF ATHENS

TIME AND SETTING

ORESTES, *maddened by the pursuit of his mother's* FURIES, *hurries from land to land trying to escape them. He comes to* APOLLO'S *sanctuary at Delphi, hoping that since it was* APOLLO *who instigated him to his act of vengeance* APOLLO *will save him. The* FURIES *meanwhile are asleep in the recesses of the shrine, exhausted by their chase. It is early afternoon.* THE PYTHIA, *an old woman, emerges into the outer court and lifts up her hands in an attitude of prayer.*

THE

EUMENIDES

THE PYTHIA

Prime in this address before the gods
I praise the Earth, primordial prophetess.
     And Themis next, the Right:
second from her mother so tradition says
to be seated on this sybil's chair.
     Third in line, another Titan:
Earth's daughter Phoebe,
who in peaceable succession without force
sat this seat and as a birthday present gave it
to Phoebus named from Phoebe:
     who left the lake on Delos with its nub of land
and beached upon these ship-trailed shores of Pallas,
coming to this country and these purlieus of Parnassus
where the children of Hephaestus[1]
(roadbuilding breed)

[1] The people of Attica.

cheered him on with pomp—
paving the lawless wilderness with law.
    Oh, how his advent made the people sing
his praises. Delphus, too,
the steerer of their state and king.
  · And Zeus breathed into Phoebus' soul the art;
sat him down as fourth upon this seer's throne.
    So Zeus it is, his father,
for whom Loxias the prophet speaks.

    These are the gods fixed in the prelude of my prayer;
with words of praise for Pallas-of-the-Holies too,
and worship for the nymphs where the hollow rock
of Corycis is bird-loud, loved
by deities that haunt.
    Bromius invests the spot (he's not forgotten)
ever since the time as god he marshaled his Bacchants
and trapped poor Pentheus to a hunted hare's demise.
    The springs of Pleistus too, and all Poseidon's power:
I call upon, with Zeus—perfector and most high.

    And so I take my throne: the prophetess.
    Now may these excel every blessing that my introit
                                                        won.
    Let any Greeks, by lot, here enter in
according to the law;
and I shall prophesy as the god leads on.

[*She goes into the temple but almost immediately comes
out again—distraught*]

    Oh, horrible to tell about—horrible to see!
Things that hurl me back again from Loxias' domain,
too weak to walk or stand;
scurrying on my hands with legs gone dumb.
    An old woman in a panic is nothing but a child.

    I was on my way
to the deep and garland-heavy shrine,
when there I see a man in God's disgrace
upon the center-stone:
sitting where the contrite sit,

hands oozing blood,
sword fresh-drawn, long olive branch
piously, enormously, bedecked with wool
as white as fleece and piercing as I saw it.

    And before that man:
the weirdest troupe of women
lolling on their seats asleep—
oh no, not women, Gorgons, surely!
or not Gorgons even but shapes like . . .
like once I saw in pictures—
carrying off the feast of Phineus—
only, these I saw were wingless, black,
absolute in their mephitic deadliness:
snoring and blowing disgustingly,
with cess of droopings leaking from their eyes; their dress
not fit to wear before the idols of the gods
nor any human home.

    I have not seen what race could spawn
such clots as these, nor any earth
that could be proud of such a breed
and not groan out in hurt and sorrow.

    But let the rest now fall to his domain:
the lord himself of here, great Loxias the strong.
    For he is health diviner, marvel reader,
and of others' homes the healing purger.

[THE PYTHIA *retires and the doors of the temple open
to disclose* ORESTES *sitting on the center-stone near the
sacred tripod, surrounded by the nodding* FURIES. *Near
him stands* APOLLO, *with* HERMES *in the background*]

APOLLO

    No—I'll not desert you, no!
    Your guardian to the end—
from a distance,
at your side:
never weak or meek towards your enemies.
    See them overcome now, these fiendish crones:
stilled into sleep, these damsels of disgust,

hoary urchin hags with whom no god can mix,
nor man nor beast—ever.

For, issued out of vice in vicious night they live
in Tartarus beneath:
a blotch of hate for both Olympian gods and men.

But you must still go fleeing
and not grow faint of heart;
for they will chase your roaming footfall far
over the steppes and constant
across the oceans even
to sea-enswirling cities.

So leave the thought behind
or tire before your time;
but when you touch upon the town of Pallas,
sit down and hug in your hands her ancient effigy.

For there'll be judges there of this
and words to charm; and we shall find a means—
an absolute release for you from all this strife:
for *I* it was who told you to take your mother's life.

ORESTES

Apollo, Lord—
so well aware of avoiding wrong—
add to your intent the not avoiding care;
so's your power for good your testimonial.

APOLLO

Remember: let no fear unseat your soul . . .
and you my brother Hermes, of my very father's blood,
look after him, true to your name: escort him,
be shepherd to my suppliant
(for God regards the outcast's rights)
into the mortal round, with happy auspices.

[APOLLO *disappears*. ORESTES *departs led by* HERMES.
The GHOST OF CLYTEMNESTRA *rises from the ground*]

CLYTEMNESTRA

Go on! Go sleeping on! We just need sleepers, eh?

so you can make this fool of me among the other dead—
among the shades where I (because of those I killed)
am a reproach that never stops wandering in my shame.
    Oh, I tell you, in their eyes—most heinously—
I am the one to blame.
    Yet even this absurd suffering from my own
makes not a single deity excite himself for me,
cut down though I am by a mother-killing son.

    See these gashes here—into my heart—from where?
    Surely in sleep your eyes can see it plain,
where the daylight blaze is dark for man's concern.
    You've sucked up quite a goodly deal from me:
with your wineless oblations, thin appeasements,
and those dead-of-nightly dinners
grilled by me in fire and sacrifice
at an hour no god shared.
    All under foot now, I see.
    All trodden down;
while *he* skips off, is gone, just like a fawn:
yes, leaps out lightly from your midst
with a merry bleat of laughter.

    Listen to me pleading for my soul.
    Awake and think, you goddesses of deep below;
for only in your dreams now is Clytemnestra calling.

> [*The* CHORUS *stirs, whimpering and
> muttering in sleep*]

Oh, whine away! The man is gone, fled far.
His friends are not at all like mine.

> [*The* CHORUS *continues to whimper and whine*]

You're too drugged with sleep. No sympathy at all.
And Orestes gone! This poor mother's murderer.

> [*The* CHORUS *moans desultorily*]

You moan and sleep. . . . Why won't you wake?
What else have you to do but stir up trouble?

> [*They moan again*]

Sleep and suffering—oh, so brilliantly conspiring!—
have altogether dimmed you down, you fiery dragoness.

[*The* FURIES *start from sleep, crying out*]

CHORUS

At him! At him! At him! At him!—Get him!

CLYTEMNESTRA

Yelping after game like silly dogs in sleep
which never can stop thinking they are on the chase.
 What are you *doing*? Get up and don't give in to toil
or let yourselves go soft with sleep and leave me in my

pain.

Whip up your livers with the lashes they deserve.
For people in the right, reproaches can be spurs.
Oh, breathe upon him with that butchery breath of

yours.

Shrivel him to ash from your smoking burning

bowels.

Off at him again. Pursue him to the bone.

[*The* GHOST OF CLYTEMNESTRA *sweeps away. The*
FURIES *begin to waken one by one*]

PARODOS [2]

Wake up! Wake up! Wake *her*
As I have woken *you*.
Asleep? Get on your feet
And let your slumbers go.
For we must see if we
Must sing an empty show.

Strophe 1

Oh, curse it! Curse it, sisters:
We have been betrayed.
And after all I've suffered,

[2] An effective way of rendering this chorus is to divide the lines
severally among individuals of each strophic group.

All of it in vain.
Oh, yes! oh, yes, we've suffered
   Through a deal of pain,
      Of hellish pain.
He's slipped out from our noose,
   Our beast he's got away.
We lost ourselves in sleep,
      And lost our prey.

Antistrophe 1

Shame! you son of Zeus
   To turn a sneak
And ride us down—us gray
   Divinities—a youth.
You cherish *him*, a beggar:
   A man God hates,
      A parent-hurter.
You snatch a matricide
   Away, and you a god.
Can anyone at all
      Call this fair?

Strophe 2

In the middle of my dreams
   I felt a scolding smite
Me hard like a horseman's goad
   Right in the midriff, right
      Under the heart.
And I am made for someone
   To beat and to benight,
      Sting and benumb:
      Ah! made to smart.

Antistrophe 2

So this is how the younger
   Gods behave and rule:
Beyond all right!
   Beads of blood on a throne

From head to foot;
And I am made to see
   Earth's center-stone
Crudely, bloodily blotched:
   Ah! made to hurt.

Strophe 3

Seer though he is he has smeared
   His very hearth himself,
Sullied his own recess:
   To flout the gods' behests,
   Promoted things of man—
Upsetting old establishments.

Antistrophe 3

Annoy me though he will
   Him I'll not unloose.
Though he flee beneath the earth
   Outlet there'll be none.
   Contrite and accursed
He shall repeat his family doom.

[APOLLO *appears from the inner sanctuary and*
confronts the FURIES]

APOLLO

Out, I say from here.
Leave this edifice at once.
Get off and gone from my prophetic holy place,
or feel the strike of a winged and coruscating snake
whipped from my golden bow,
to make you froth away your life in spasms
of black and man-drawn bile—
spewing out your clotted human suckings.

This is no fitting residence for you to board.
Yours is a place of sentences:
where heads are chopped, eyes gouged, throats cut,
and seed is crushed from striplings spoiled in flower.

Yes, a place of mutilations, stonings—
helpless wailings long drawn out
from men pinned through the spine.

Do you want to know what turns the stomachs of the
Gods?

Those feasts you find so charming.
Your whole shape and mien give you away.
Freaks like you should make their hole
deep in some blood-beslobbered lion's den
and not come rubbing off their filth
on those beside these sacred mantic spots.

Get gone, you goatish rabble with no goatherd:
No god's love is lost on such a flock.

CHORUS

My lord Apollo,
you must take your turn to listen too:
for no mere accessory of this
but perpetrator absolute, arch-criminal, are you.

CHORUS *and* APOLLO

AP: How's that? Explain exactly what you say.

CH: It was *you* arranged this traveling matricide.

AP: Arrangement for a vengeance of a father: yes—
what then?

CH: And then you made yourself receiver of spilt blood.

AP: I sent him for his purging to this very house.

CH: While we who spurred him on, we are the ones
abused.

AP: You took the liberty of coming near my home.

CH: But that precisely is the part we were assigned.

AP: Your part and special privilege, eh? Oh, boast it
out.

CH: Murderers of mothers we harry from their homes.

AP: Then what about a woman who undermines her
                                                    man?

CH: Such a killing does not count as blood of kin.

APOLLO

How you heap contempt upon—make cheap—
Hera's consummated pact with Zeus.
  Aphrodite too such logic brushes off, condemns—
the source of mankind's sweetest joys.
  Love in marriage is a holy state between a man and
                                                    woman:
stronger than an oath, sentineled by Right.
  And if one slays the other and you be lax,
not flash in anger on them,
I'll never for a moment say you are not wrong
to hunt Orestes down.
  Your passion for the one is all too plain,
as slackness and remiss are blazoned in the other.
  But Pallas shall preside in this: the goddess, judge.

CHORUS *and* APOLLO

CH: Never shall I leave that man alone.

AP: Go on then, chase—and pile your troubles up.

CH: You shan't lop short my privileges with talk.

AP: Your privileges! I would not take them as a gift.

CHORUS

No: for you are altogether perfect, so they say,
at Zeus's throne.
  But I'll pursue my suit,
and I am on the scent
of mother's blood
with justice for this man.

APOLLO

And I shall hurry to his side and save my client.
For under heaven and earth no anger is so deep
as a postulant's who's spurned—
if from him I let myself be turned.

[APOLLO *disappears into the sanctuary. The scene shifts
to the Acropolis at Athens, in the temple of* PALLAS
ATHENA. ORESTES *is ushered in by* HERMES; *he seizes
and embraces the ancient statue of* ATHENA. *Several
weeks, even months, have passed, long enough for* ORES-
TES *to have wandered to many places expiating his sin.
Though he still wears the modest dress of a suppliant, it
is no longer blood-stained*]

ORESTES

Pallas Athena, Princess,
Apollo sent me here—a stricken man.
    Be kind and shelter me.
    I need no cleansing now:
come not with dripping hands,
but guilt ground down—already worn away—
on others' thresholds: the thoroughfares of men.

    Persevering over land and sea,
keeping everything that Loxias in oracles enjoined,
I come before your house, great goddess, and your
                                                image;
and here I'll watch and wait till the issue of my trial.

[*The* FURIES *hurry in one by one
                searching and scenting*]

CHORUS

Aha! here it is here:
clear traces of the man.
    Follow them up,
those bright and silent pointers.

Like a dog on a wounded fawn
we track him by red trickles.
Though we are worn to nothing:
inhumanly diminished.

We pant our souls away,
ranging every region.
Wingless over the sea we've chased
swiftly as a frigate.

And now at last he's here—
somewhere cowering.
How I chuckle at the smell
of human bleeding.

Look, look again, explore
Every spot and stop him slipping
    Away—a matricide.

Ah! there he is once more:
Sheltering—arms entwined
Round the statue of the goddess,
For his sin, and begging
    Trial and acquittal.

But *that* may not be:
A mother's blood once spilt
    Is passed recall.
Oh, that flood on the floor
    Has gushed and gone!

In requite I'll suck
    Your limbs alive
    Of scarlet chrism;
And you must let me.

Oh, to feed on you—
You grisly elixir!
And when I've sucked you limp
I'll drag you down
    Below to pay
A murdered mother's pains.

And there you'll see the rest

Of them that sinned
Against a godhead or a guest
Or loving parents wronged:
Each to each his proper punishment.

Yes, Hades is a master
    Auditor of men
    Once down below,
Where all accounts are tableted
    Deep in his gaze.

ORESTES

Oh, evil's hit me hard and now I know
all the rubrics of the purge: when to speak,
when likewise to be still.
    And in this present instance a wise preceptor says:
Speak out.

For the blood on my hands is sleeping, paling.
That horrid spot of mother's gore now washes out.
In its first freshness even, it was cleansed
at Apollo's hearth by sacrifice of swine . . .
but that would take too long to tell (how it began,
and those I conversed with and never harmed) . . . .
    Ah! Time in passing washes out the past.

But now from a rinsed and holy mouth
I call upon this country's queen—
    Athena: come and save me!
    Not a spear to be raised, and she shall win me:
yes—my self, my land, my people, Argos . . .
friends fit and staunch—allies forever.

So, be she in Libya somewhere: its purlieus and places;
around her own stream: the runneling Triton;
be her foot lifted rampant (or quiet)
in succor to friends;
or she like a man and a leader of men,
standing surveying the Phlegraean plain—
    Oh, may she come!
(for she hears like a goddess afar)

and let her unloosen me free.

CHORUS

Not Apollo, not all Athena's power,
can snatch you from abandonment and ruin:
a spirit absolutely ignorant of joy—
bloodless fodder for the demons; and a shade.

> [*The* FURIES *wait for some response*]

What! won't you answer?
Not repudiate these words of mine?
Sweet victim fattened for me!
Banquet all alive—oblated at no altar! . . .
Then listen spellbound to this song.

> [*The* FURIES *begin to dance and sing
> in a weird measure*]

FIRST STASIMON

Come, link hands and join the dance
　　Of hate in the canticle
Blasted by us with the best of intent
To give you a lesson on how the lots
Are issued to men by our committee.
　　　　Oh, we're so fair
　　　　So very proper!

Hold out your hands and if they are clean
You are safe from ambush, safe from our spleen,
　　To live your lifetime safe from harm.
But if they are crimson (creatures like *him*:
　　Criminal hands behind a back),
We'll stand right up and show the slain,
Change ourselves and make it plain:
　　We're the unflagging avengers.

Strophe 1

　O mother who bore me, Night my mother,
　* To plague and punish the quick and the dead,
　　Leto's son would do me dishonor.

For listen: he's whisking away
This little huddled rabbit—
Beautifully fit to atone
    A murdered mother.

Refrain 1

Over the victim set for the fire
Sing a song of madness, sing
Frenzy and horror to harrow the brain.
    Chant of the Furies chain
    The mind with your lyreless charm
      And shrivel the heart.

Antistrophe 1

For this is the lot that Moira spun
Ruthlessly for our ruthless keeping:
When there falls on a man the reckless sin
    Of self-destroying his kin,
    We dog him down under the earth
    To his minikin freedom of death—
      Hardly excessive.

Refrain 1

Over the victim set for the fire
Sing a song of madness, sing
Frenzy and horror to harrow the brain.
    Chant of the Furies chain
    The mind with your lyreless charm
      And shrivel the heart.

Strophe 2

This was the settlement made us—our lot when begot:
Hands off Immortals and no collocations of banquets;
Nothing in common and nothing at all of the whiteness
    They wear on their feast days:
      The staggering whiteness.[3]

[3] A short last line of seven syllables seems to be missing from
the Greek. I have supplied it by slightly expanding the connotation of
the original.

Refrain 2

But ours is to topple the houses
Where Ares the house pet has turned
And taken a bite out of love.
So we swoop on this man though he's strong,
We waste him away for the blood
    So freshly sprung.

Antistrophe 2

We hasten to arrogate all to ourselves this commission;
And remove from the gods any competence over our
                                          counsels;
Not even a trial, since Zeus considers above 'bomination
    Our converse: this blood-
      Dripping band's.

Refrain 2

But ours is to topple the houses
Where Ares the house pet has turned
And taken a bite out of love.
So we swoop on this man though he's strong,
We waste him away for the blood
    So freshly sprung.

Strophe 3

And all the highest opinions of men under heaven
    Melt into earth and trivially dwindle
    When mantled in black we attack
    With the beat of our feet in our hating.

Refrain 3

Smack! with a leap from above
I crash down my foot with a fall
Heavy from high with limbs a-fly—
To trip you swift runner to ruin!

Antistrophe 3

But blind to his fall he is drunk with the lees of his folly:
Such is the cloud of infection that floats
On the man; and a fog-full of rumors
Crowd on his house, crying sorrow.

Refrain 3

Smack! with a leap from above
I crash down my foot with a fall
Heavy from high with limbs a-fly—
To trip you swift runner to ruin!

Strophe 4

So it's fixed and we follow it through
With resource, for we never forget
A single mistake; we're stern—
Implacably strict with men.
Dishonored, despised, we do
Our duty (though barred from the gods
With a sunless torch): to roughen the road
For eyes that are dark and that see.

Antistrophe 4

So who in the world would not worry
Or wince with awe when he hears
We're ordained to this order by Fate,
Vowed to devotion by gods?
Divinely we hold to our work
Given of old. And respect
Is ours although under the earth
We're stationed in sunless murk.

[PALLAS ATHENA *sweeps in
flourishing her shield*]

ATHENA

Far away I heard a voice that called me,
far off as Scamander:

land I claim as certainly bestowed me
by the Grecian lords and leaders—
that generous portion of the spoil their spears won,
bequeathed me root and branch as mine forever:
chosen legacy to Theseus' sons. . . .

I swept from there, on swift feet came,
winged by my hurricane shield a-flutter
full with the wind like harnessed horses.[4]

But what vision in the land is this?
This extraordinary array?
Which does not make me quake with fear but blink
                                        with wonder!
Who in the world are you? The lot of you, I mean?
This stranger sitting at my statue's feet?
And you—you spawn of race unclassified,
unglimpsed among the goddesses by gods,
not even stamped from any human mold? . . .
but no, it is not fair to be unkind
in the presence of a freak—[5]
fairness stands aloof.

CHORUS

Daughter of Zeus, you shall hear it all in brief:
we are the dismal children of Night—
called curses in the deep abodes beneath.

ATHENA *and* CHORUS

AT: A race I know: oh, names notorious!

CH: You'll quickly come to learn our functions too.

AT: Why, certainly, if your account be plain.

---

[4] This line (405): πώλοις ἀκμαίοις τόνδ' ἐπιζεύξασ' ὄχον, is omitted by
some editors on the grounds that Athena has just said she came on
foot, not by chariot. Perhaps it was interpolated into later stagings of
the play when Athena is made to arrive by chariot. I have taken a
liberty and amalgamated the two possibilities (and possibly have
achieved what Aeschylus intended).

[5] I take the reading ἄμορφον (deformed) rather than ἄμομφον (innocent). It has more point.

CH: Slayers of men we hurtle from their homes.

AT: Where to? What is the limit to a slayer's flight?

CH: Where the word for happiness is nowhere known.

AT: So this man here is victim of your hue and cry?

CH: Of course! He set himself the murdering of his
                                                    mother.

AT: What made him do it? What fear or force?

CH: Is *any* motive good enough to goad to matricide?

AT: The question has two sides: you speak for only
                                                    one.

CH: But he'll not take an oath nor tender one.

AT: Not justice, then, is what *you* want, but just the
                                                    form.

CH: How so? Explain. You lack no cleverness.

AT: I say: legality must never make wrong right.

CH: Then cross-examine him yourself and judge.

AT: You truly want to lay the case with me?

CH: Why not? From noble lineage cherish noble law.

ATHENA

[turning to ORESTES]

Stranger, your turn now:
and what have you to say?
   Tell me first your country, race and fortunes;
then defend yourself against this charge—
if you really think your case is sound,
which makes you sit here by my hearth and hug my
                                                    form:
a dedicated penitent like Ixion.
   Give me some assurance of these things.

ORESTES

Sovereign Athena,
first from your last words
I would remove a mighty slur:
I am no contaminated suppliant
clinging to your effigy with dirty hands.
   I'll give you proof of this—a weighty proof.

The man of blood keeps mute, the canons say,
until he is sprinkled with a yeanling sacrificed
by one who is fit to wash his blood away.
   Victims and running streams,
these rites at other seats I have fulfilled:
this care at least I clear from off our way.

And now, to tell you quickly of my origins:
I am an Argive, and my father—your question honors

                                me—

was Agamemnon, admiral of the fleet,
with whom you toppled down the Trojan town of Troy.
   He came back home, but not to a noble end.
   My black-hearted mother butchered him,
enveloped him in broidered toils—
screaming out their witness:
   "Oh, murder in a bath!"

And I returning home—an exile then—
cut her down the killer, oh, I'll not say "no,"
in forfeit for my father's blood I loved.
   But Apollo was a party to it too.
   He pricked me on with threats if I should fail
to do the deed on her who owes.

For right or wrong you are my judge:
I'll bow before your verdict
whichever way it goes.

ATHENA

This matter is too grave for any man to take upon
                                 himself;

and even I cannot decide in cases of hot blood—
especially since you've cast yourself (with ritual care)
harmless and annealed, as a suppliant on my house.

I receive you therefore in my city unaccused.

Yet, these women have a work we cannot slight
and if they fail to be victorious in this,
the poison of their disappointment afterwards
will drop infection on the ground
and blight our earth with everlasting plague.

The dilemma's that: dismiss or let them stay?
Either course will hurt; is difficult for me.
But since on me this suit has come to rest,
I shall elect, and have sworn in, a court of homicide:
a lasting tribunal for time to come.

So call your proofs and witnesses,
sworn evidence to sway your cause.
And when I've singled out my best of citizens
I shall return and set them fairly to the proof,
bound by an oath against a word against the truth.

[PALLAS ATHENA *departs*]

CHORUS

Strophe 1—Second Stasimon

Now is paramount the new
Rebellion of the laws if this
Mother's murderer and crime—
His cause—shall come to triumph.

Oh, how the ease of it soon shall match
Every man to his callous bent:
Again and again the murderous stroke
Shall lurk for parents in days to come,
Ah! which children's hands have dealt.

Antistrophe 1

And we who watch on mortal man,
We the furious ones aflame,

Shall loose no anger on his crime;
For bursts of neuter death shall rain.

Prompting each other each shall know
How his own demise is near:
The plunge of his end away from harm.
Oh, unconsoled and fearful man—
What a useless cure to own!

Strophe 2

Nevermore let any call
Fatally when he is down,
Pouring out this anguished groan:
    "O Justice come!
O, Furies', Furies' thrones!"

So might a father wail
And so a wounded mother:
Sorrow on sorrows now
The House of Justice falls.

Antistrophe 2

There is a time for fear
To sit inside the will;
To guard and there preside.
    Oh, it is good
To groan and so be wise.

How might a man not trained
In fear of heart—a man
Or city too—still learn
Respect for Righteousness?

Strophe 3

The life which has no law,
The life which is a slave's,
    Be far from praise.
God gives power to modesty
But other things to others.
And this, my truth corroborates:

For pride is the certain child
Of a life unprincipled.
But from the soul's own sanity
      Comes happiness
      The world's desire
      The many-cherishèd.

Antistrophe 3

I say to you in all:
To bow before the shrine
      Of Right; not let
Your lusting eyes for gain
Ungod your foot against her,
Or punishments will follow:
The end will fit the cause.
So let a man first serve
His parents filiality;
      Then to those
      Who gather in his house
      A reverent amiability.

Strophe 4

He who is *willingly* just (not by constraint)
   Shall never be left unblessed
Or lost with all his portion overthrown.
   Ah! but the swaggering sinner, I say,
   Who ransacks right pell mell with wrong,
   Shall one day have to strike his sail
      In the strain of the jib and the squall,
      With shattered yardarm gone.

Antistrophe 4

Pleading his sound-lost calls he's caught in the deep
      Unassailable swirls. The laugh
Of the gods is gay at the sight of this desperate man,
   No longer the braggart but bound and pressed
   In the comb of unmountable crests:
   He and all his original luck
      Swept on the rock of the Right

Unwitnessed—away—unwept.

[*The scene changes to the council hall of the Areopagus
(also on the Acropolis), where* PALLAS ATHENA *enters
at the head of twelve* JURYMEN *who take their seats.*
ORESTES *removes to the dock. Behind him is a great
crowd of people. The* HERALD *holds a trumpet in readiness*]

ATHENA

Announce, herald! Announce! and hold the concourse
back.
Let the Tuscan trumpet pierce and swell with human
breath,
as it strains its clarion summons to the concourse called
which swells into the council hall. Let silence reign,
that all the city hear forevermore what I ordain
and these litigants see just judgment here obtain.

[*The trumpet blares, the people settle,
and* APOLLO *enters*]

CHORUS

Lord Apollo, keep within your own domain.
What part in this affair is yours, explain?

APOLLO

Why, I've come as a witness—
the accused sat at my hearth, was duly at my shrine,
it was I who purged him of this bloody act—
his witness and his advocate;
that bloody act against his mother's, mine.

[*Turns to* ATHENA]

Proceed please with the trial.
Preside as you know how.

ATHENA

[*Addressing the* FURIES]

The floor is yours. I introduce the trial.

Prosecutor's privilege is to state the case—
unfold it from the first.

CHORUS

Many are we, but straight to the point.
Answer us word for word and one by one.
First: your mother—did you kill her?

ORESTES *and* CHORUS

OR: I did, and do not in the least deny it.

CH: Aha! the first round goes to us: the first of three.

OR: You crow before your man is down.

CH: Then suppose you tell us how you killed her?

OR: I say: I took my sword and ran her through the
throat.[5b]

CH: On whose suggestion? Who planned the thing?

OR: This selfsame prophet-god. He'll answer for me.

CH: What! a god and prophet prompt to matricide?

OR: Yes. And to this moment I do not blame my lot.

CH: Ah! when the sentence grips you, you'll change
your tone.

OR: I am confident. My father'll send his help beyond
the grave.

CH: So—kill a mother, all to trust a corpse!

OR: I do. She smeared herself twice over with her sin.

CH: Precisely how? Please tell the judges that.

OR: The stroke that slayed her husband felled my father.

CH: She paid for it and died: *you* still live.

[5b] Aeschylus has already made the ghost of Clytemnestra say that she
was "gashed in the heart." Either he has forgotten this or the phrase
πρὸς δέρην τεμών ("cut upon or toward the neck") can be legitimately
translated as "thrust up to the hilt": δέρη can in fact mean "ridge,"
so perhaps "hilt." The sentence would then be: "I took my sword and
ran it to the hilt."

OR: But when she lived why didn't you pursue and
                                      pounce?

CH: Because she was not one blood with the man she
                                      killed.

OR: But I and my mother *am* one blood presumably?

CH: Red murderer, you are! How else nurtured
                          underneath her zone?
       Would you disclaim that sweetest closeness of a
                          mother's blood?

ORESTES

[*Turning to* APOLLO]

Now give testimony for me, Apollo, and expound.
Was I justified in killing her?
It happened as it did; there's no denying.
But in your judgment was it right or wrong—
this deed of blood?
Decide; that I can tell the court.

APOLLO

[*Turning to the jury*]

I shall tell you honestly—
you, this high tribunal of Athena—
for a seer cannot deceive.

Never once have I spoken from my mantic seat,
on man or maid or state,
a syllable that Zeus has not enjoined—
the Father of Olympus.
Such is justice at its strongest—mark it well.
I am asking you to bow before the Father's will.
No oath exists more binding-strong than Zeus.[6]

---

[6] Meaning that their oath to give a verdict according to the evidence
may have to yield to the higher principle of Divine mercy.

CHORUS

So Zeus, you say, was prompter of this oracle,
bidding this man Orestes to avenge his father's blood
by ignoring every scrap of honor to his mother?

APOLLO

These are not the same:
a great man was murdered here,
divinely rich in sceptered rule,
and murdered by a woman—
not by some gallant Amazon's
arrows sped from far
(as might have been),
but as you shall hear, Athena;
and all of you in solemn session
who vote upon this cause.

He came back from the wars,
crowned with some success his subjects said,
and she received him kindly;
then, in his bath,
flung on him a tented cloak:
caught him rim to rim,
bedizened him in a maze of folds—
hewed down her man.

Ah! a great man down—precisely as I tell it—
admired by all and admiral of the fleet . . .
but this woman I have shown for what she was,
to make you people rage who try this cause.

CHORUS

Zeus, you say, puts greater stock upon a father's end,
yet he himself put chains on *his* old father, Cronus.
How does this not contradict?
I call upon the court to witness.

APOLLO

You unlovable brutes, you gods' aversion:
shackles can be loosed; they have a cure—
oh, many a device to shake them free;
but let the dust soak up the blood of man once dead,
there's no reraising it.
    For this, my father did not fashion any spell,
though otherwise he turns at will
the whole world upside down
and never pants for toil.

CHORUS

See where it leads to if you let this man go free!
the very one who poured his mother's life's blood on

                            the ground
goes off to live in Argos in his father's home.
    What public altars can he visit now?
What brotherhood will let him have ablution?

APOLLO

This too I shall explain,
and you will see that I am right:

    The mother is not parent of her so-called child
but only nurse of the new-sown seed.
    The man who puts it there is parent;
she merely cultivates the shoot—
    host for a guest—if no god blights.

    I shall give you proof of what I say.
There can be fatherhood without a mother.
The living truth stands there:

                    [*Points to* PALLAS ATHENA]

the daughter of Olympian Zeus—
never nurtured in the darkness of a womb,
a shoot no goddess struck.

Ah, Pallas, in this as everything,
I do my best to make your town and people great.
This man I sent as suppliant to your home
to engender loyalty in him forever,
so, goddess, let you gain
a fighting friend with all his race to come,
and make this covenant go lasting down
blessed by this people and posterity.

ATHENA

Is it time for me to put the jury to the vote—
for their honest verdict—has enough been said?

CHORUS

We've shot out every weapon that we have
and only wait to hear the issue of the trial.

ATHENA

Indeed! But how shall *I* behave and be unblamed?

APOLLO

You've heard what you've heard,
and as you cast your votes
drop in your hearts some fealty to oaths.

ATHENA

Listen now to my statute, you men of Attica,
you who judge in this first of murder trials:

This bench and this tribunal in the future
is perpetually set up for Aegeus' people.
On this hill of Ares, seat and camp of Amazons
who came surging battle-hot on Theseus
and raised new citadels of towers
high to rival his,
and sacrificed to Ares,
and gave this rock its name: "Areopagus"—

the "Hill of Ares" . . .
    On this hill, I say,
the devotion of my people linked with holy fear
shall keep them day and night all free from wrong
so long as they, the citizens, will not discolor
their laws with any dirty draft . . .
for once the clear stream is mixed with mud
you'll never find a drink.

    Neither lawlessness nor dictatorship
would I have my people furbish or respect,
nor yet send fear entirely packing from the town:
what human being uncurbed by fear is just?
    With such a holy fear, and such a justice, then,
you have a bulwark for your land and safety for your
                                                    city
as has no other race of man—
neither in Scythia nor in Pelops' place.

    Venerable, not venal,
this tribunal I establish now:
quick to vengeance and alert—
a sentry over sleep.

    Such the exhortation I extend forever to my people.
    Rise up now, assume your ballots, vote your verdicts,
and each respect his oath;
my harangue is done.

[*The* JURORS *drop their ballots one by one into the two
urns, either of bronze for acquittal, or of wood for
condemnation*]

CHORUS

    I advise you not to disregard our sisterhood:
we can be a heavy load upon your land.

APOLLO

    And my oracles—which are those of Zeus—I ask you:
do not ignore or make them fruitless.

CHORUS

Oh, you and your concern with blood beyond your
business!
the prophecies you prophesy are tainted now.

APOLLO

So my Father made an error in his judgment
when Ixion, first murderer, appealed to him?

CHORUS

You talk. But if I fail to win my cause
I shall come back and haunt this land.

APOLLO

You are of no consequence either among the elder
or the younger gods. . . . I shall win.

CHORUS

And in Pheres' house you did the same:
talked the Fates to letting men off death.

APOLLO

And is it wrong to reward a worshiper,
especially when he stands in need of help?

CHORUS

But *you* upset the ancient principalities
and overcame old goddesses with wine.

APOLLO

And *you* are presently going to lose your case
and spit out venom—but devoid of virulence.

CHORUS

Well, since you ride me down—old age a youth—
I can only wait the outcome of this trial,
my anger wavering still against this town.

[*As the twelfth* AREOPAGITE *drops his pebble
into the voting urn,* ATHENA *rises*]

ATHENA

My business is to close the case:
my own vote goes in favor of Orestes.

No mother ever gave me birth:
I am unreservedly for male in everything
save marrying one—
enthusiastically on my father's side.
I cannot find it in me to prefer
the fate of a wife who slew her man:
the master of the house.

If the votes are even, then Orestes wins.
Toss out the ballots from the urns with all dispatch,
you jurors to whom this office falls.

ORESTES *and* CHORUS

OR: Phoebus Apollo—how will the verdict go?

CH: Black Night my mother—are you looking on?

OR: This is the end: a noose or the full clear day.

CH: We are finished, or firmly hold our own.

APOLLO

Pour out the ballotings with care, my friends.
Separate them with a scrupulous rectitude.
A trifling error can become a great calamity.
The cast of a single vote has saved a house.

[*The ballots are counted and shown to* ATHENA]

ATHENA

This man stands acquitted on a charge of blood:
the number of the votes is equal.

[APOLLO *slips away*]

ORESTES

[*Coming forward and throwing himself before the goddess*]

O, Pallas Athena, you have saved my house:
I was stripped of my country and you gave me home.
    At last a Greek can say:
"He is an Argive once again,
housed on his father's heritage."

    Yes, by the grace of Pallas and Apollo,
and of that third great universal Providence
which looked to my father's death,
saw what advocates my mother has . . .
and saves me so.

    Now I depart for home,
with an everlasting promise to this state and people:
    Never shall a princeling of my land
set out with furbished spear against you.
    Rather from the grave, I shall myself
stir up dismay and accident on those who break this

oath:

dog their marches with discouragement,
put sinister auguries in their way
and make them sorry for their pains.
    But while these oaths are kept—
to those who cherish this city of Pallas with a friendly

lance,

to them I shall be more than kind.

    Farewell then to you, and this great civilian throng.
    Hold down your enemies in a grip they cannot tear,
with championship and safety carried on your spear.

[ORESTES *departs*]

CHORUS

Strophe 1

Curse on you upstart gods who have ridden
Down immemorial laws and filched them
Clean from my fingers. Abused, disappointed,
   Raging I come—oh, shall come!—
    And drip from my heart
  A hurt on your soil, a contagion,
   A culture, a canker:
Leafless and childless Revenge
Rushing like wildfire over the lowlands,
Smearing its death-pus on mortals and meadows.

  Shall I cry—oh, cry for the future?
   Mocked by these burghers!
   Insufferably worsted!
  Bitter Night's daughters, immensely
   Dishonored and saddened.

ATHENA

Let me persuade you not to break your heart so:
you *were* not beaten; the votes were only even;
all fell fair and no disgrace to you.
  Testimony flooded like a light from Zeus;
the seer himself gave evidence
that Orestes be not hurt for what he did.
So, forget your fury and forbear from hurling
your loaded hate upon this land;
nor make it barren
with that acid rain of death
which eats and wastes the tender seeds.

  I pledge to you in absolute good faith
a cavernous deep place—your rightly promised land.
  There you shall sit by hearths on shining thrones;
and by these selfsame citizens
most abundantly be worshiped.

CHORUS

Antistrophe 1

Curse on you upstart gods who have ridden
Down immemorial laws and filched them
Clean from my fingers. Abused, disappointed,
   Raging I come—oh, shall come!—
    And drip from my heart
  A hurt on your soil, a contagion,
    A culture, a canker:
Leafless and childless Revenge
Rushing like wildfire over the lowlands,
Smearing its death-pus on mortals and meadows.

Shall I cry—oh, cry for the future?
  Mocked by these burghers!
  Insufferably worsted!
Bitter Night's daughters, immensely
  Dishonored and saddened.

ATHENA

But you are *not* dishonored.
Goddesses so wild with anger, do not wreck a world
                       of men.

I too believe in Zeus; but need I tell you?
  I alone of the gods am privy to the keys of chambers
where the locked-up thunder lies . . .
but no need of that!—only listen to me:
do not scatter on the world
words from a madcap tongue
and make all fruitfulness a barren thing.
  Let your bitter-black and raging combers sleep,
and you shall be revered with pride and live with me.
  And when the rich and many first fruits of this
                   ample land
are yours forever—
offerings for births and for betrothals—
you shall praise my reasons then.

CHORUS

Strophe 2

That *I* could be so beaten!
I the old wisdom under the earth
Displaced like dirt!
My very breath is caught with fury and disgust.
Earth, the disgrace!
Oh, what is this pain—seeping through my sides?
Mother, I am hurt.
O hear me Night.
They have stripped me down, the gods:
Tricked all my status from me.

ATHENA

I'll bear with your anger, for you are elder
and therefore certainly more wise than I;
but Zeus gave me a mind as well:
this other-peopled land you've come to
you shall learn to love—I so predict it.
And, onward rolling time shall roll the honors on
these citizens of mine;
and you shall be installed in glory by Erechtheus' shrine
with such trains of men and women worshiping
as you could never win yourselves from all the world
beside.

So, in these my realms you must not throw
your bloody whetstone down
to sharpen up and spoil the spleen of youth
with passions worse than wine;
or snatch the hearts from fighting cocks
and bury them with Ares deep amongst my citizens
made savage on each other.
Keep war outside and far from home—
keep it for the greedy of hard-won fame.
Battle with the home-bred bird . . . I do not name.

These are the choices proffered at my hand:
high deserts, high deeds, high honors—

shared in this god-beloved land.

CHORUS

Antistrophe 2

That *I* could be so beaten!
I the old wisdom under the earth
Displaced like dirt!
My very breath is caught with fury and disgust.
Earth, the disgrace!
Oh, what is this pain—seeping through my sides,
Mother, I am hurt.
Oh, hear me, Night.
They have stripped me down, the gods:
Tricked all my status from me.

ATHENA

I shall not tire of tempting you with good,
and you shall never say that you—
uncivilly and scorned—
were ousted from this land by me,
old goddess by a new,
and by my mortal citizens.

No, if you'll but recognize the holy power of Peitho
in the sweet beguilement of my tongue,
then indeed you'll stay.
But if you do not wish to stay,
it would surely be unfair of you
to weight this city down with wrath, revenge, or wrong
against my people.
It rests with you to be a princeling of these parts
and have a fair, full measure of its homage.

CHORUS *and* ATHENA

CH: Lady Athena, what is this place for me you speak
of?

AT: One innocent of pain. Take it for your own.

CH: And if I do, what privilege is in store?

AT: No single house shall thrive except by you.

CH: But will you really work it that I wax so strong?

AT: Yes; for we bless the fortunes of our votaries.

CH: And what assurance can you give—everlastingly?

AT: I am not the one to pledge and not perform.

CH: You are winning me, I think: my anger goes.

AT: On this soil—stay here: you'll have other friends
                                                besides.

CH: Ah, this soil! what wishes for it would you have
                                                me hymn?

ATHENA

        Never to see wrong right,
but blessings from the earth
and from the deep sea drifts;
and out of the sky
winds and breezes blowing
clear sunshine on the soil;
and overflowing plenty
of fruit and field and flock,
which fails our people never;
and precious life
for man's own mortal seed;
the wicked weeded out—
for like a careful gardener
I love my plants:
this race of just and harmless men.

        Such *your* part; and mine:
never to allow
this city in the dazzling lists of war
not to be conquest-crowned in the world of men
and not to be distinct.

CHORUS

Strophe 1—Third Stasimon

I will have a home with Pallas,

Not disgrace this city,
Which Zeus all-ruling—Ares too—
Makes the gods' own garrison:
Guarded jewel and perfect shrine of Hellas' deities.
For her I make my prayer
With generous prophecy:
That from the swelling earth shall burst
A beam of life
By the glorious beat of the sun.

ATHENA

Thus with a will, thus dispatching
This for these citizens, I'm investing
Divinities for them great and exacting:
Everything human falls to their function,
And anyone failing
To feel their import
Does not know whence life can hit him.
The sins of the fathers draw a man near them
Till destruction
Without a sound levels him down
Loudly boasting:
Viciously, angrily, into the dust.

CHORUS

Antistrophe 1

Let no blasting wind blight trees:
This the grace I utter.
Let no hotness blaze across
And scorch away the buddings.
Let no thwarting canker creep, blistering the fruitings.
But may Earth engender
In her lavish season
Twofold yeanlings to the flocks;
A stream of fortunes from the mines,
God-blessèd and god-given.

ATHENA

Do you hear it, my watchmen, what she accomplishes?

Great is the power of the formidable Lady
Erinyes: both with the undying deities
And with the beings below; but with men—
Manifest, absolute, working her will:
Holding a song out to some; and to others
 Only a life bemisted with tears.

CHORUS

Strophe 2

Away with the murder of man
Upset before his prime,
And *on* with the marriage of maidens
All-lovely, matched with man—
 O you whose office it is!
On with it goddesses, Fates,
Sisters of ours through our mother.
Grant it you spirits upright—
Confessed in every home,
Gravid at every season
With every visit deserved . . .
O grant it, august of the gods!

ATHENA

How it delights me: this will and this promise
 Of yours for my country!
The eyes of Persuasion—how I adore them
For watching over my lips and my tongue
When pitted against your so wild opposition.
But Zeus has prevailed: the god of forensic.
 Our passion for good
 Wins out at the last.

CHORUS

Antistrophe 2

Rebellion, that ravenous horror,
Never must rear on the city
Its hideous roar, I beseech;

And never the dust drink up
The dark of the people's blood
(Gulping vendettas down):
Slaughter for slaughter and ruin
Raging over the town.
Reciprocate graces instead
With mutual notions of love
And a single one of hate:
Such is the cure for much among men.

ATHENA

Oh, you are wise, now you discover
    The way to speak kindly.
And now as I gaze on these formidable faces,
Great is the gain I foresee for this people:
Blest by the blessèd and paying high worship
Always, and steering the land and the city
    Straight for the right
Onwards with honors forever.

CHORUS

Strophe 3

Farewell and farewell, with largess for your lot!
    Farewell, you men of this city:
        Seated by Zeus,[7]
    Loved by the virgin beloved,
    Learning discernment at last
    Under the wings of Athena
    And great in the eyes of her father.

[*While the following verses are sung,* PALLAS ATHENA *stations herself at the head of the* FURIES—*now propitiously renamed the* EUMENIDES *or Gentle Ones. At the same time an escort of matrons, girls, and grandmothers—the* CHORUS *of* ATHENIAN WOMEN—*forms for the grand processional exit*]

---

7 Reference to a local sanctuary on the Areopagus dedicated to Olympian Zeus.

ATHENA

And farewell to *you*; but first by the holy light
    Of this escort and marching before you
    I mean to show you your chambers.
    Oh, go majestically sped,
With these holocausts, under the ground. Hold off
    All harm against this country:
Sending whatever is gain for the town
      To crown her with conquests.
You children of Cranaüs, abiding polity,
Lead away these our latest incumbents,
With goodness for good in the heart of our people.

CHORUS

Antistrophe 3

    Farewell and farewell! I must shout it again:
      A paean to all in the city,
      Both tutelary spirits and men,
      Who live in these purlieus of Pallas.
      Cherish my presence amongst you,
      So will you find in your lives
        Nothing to blame.

ATHENA

    Praised be the words of your prayers.
And now with the light of these torch-flung flames,
I take you down to the deeps of the underworld
With this ministrant escort—women devoted
    To watching my image.

Oh, let these apples of Theseus' eye,
Glory of this land, come forth:
Girls and matrons, muster of dames,
    Apparelled in purple for honor.

Let the torches blaze and begin,
That this bountiful fellowship come to our plot
Shine on the future with man-happy lot.

[*The procession begins to move off. The* EUMENIDES
*are led down the steps of the temple towards their
shrines under the earth*]

GRAND CHORUS OF ATHENIAN WOMEN

ESCORT

Go to your homes you adorers of greatness:
Triumph attend you old children—no children—of Night.

ALL

And bless them you people.

ESCORT

Into the primal crypts of the earth:[8]
Bedizened and burning with sacrifice, honor and worship . . . .

ALL

Oh, one and all bless them!

ESCORT

Bland and benign to our land, go forth,
With the celebrate torches' glow on your path:
You venerable divas be gay.

ALL

And raise a hurrah with your song.

8 The Eumenides had their sanctuaries in dark chapels lit by
lamps under the Hill of Ares.

ESCORT

Pour out a fellowship in perpetuity
  Made with these guests and these people of Pallas,
  Which Zeus the All-seeing, with Fate, has confirmed.

ALL

Raise a hurrah with your song.

[*The procession,* ATHENA *leading,*
                          winds out of sight]

APPENDIX I

TRANSLATOR'S INTENTIONS

It might be thought that Aeschylus should be translated with a slightly stiff and formal quality, something with a liturgical flavor, or something a little bit Miltonian, to match the measured division of his lines in Greek. My answer is that the grandeur of Aeschylus is more often Shakespearean than Miltonian, stiffened with a heavy shot of Marlowe. It flashes with concentrated brilliances of sense and sound, and advances with a pounding impetus. Compared to Sophocles, his poetry is less subtle but more vivid, heightened, and swift; compared to Euripides, it is more robust. It might be thought that he could be rendered in a kind of Racine grand manner: in a tight, ordered language, architectonic, horizontally as firm as the Parthenon, magnificently spare. This too, I think, would be a mistake. The grand manner is undoubtedly there, but it is very different from Racine's. It floods and pours, almost in an excess of language, is loose-limbed, unpredictable, and leaps with a vertical resilience.

In my own effort to catch some of it I have sought a line which is variable, nimble, and elastic but which never departs from an unmistakable measure and beat. I have not, in this, felt tempted to the view that translating is a craft and should be systematized and approached in a scientific state of mind. It is true that machines, reared on a strict system, are now doing this, but for me translating is an art; and in art it is not by striving after identity that one thing is made to reveal another but by a resolution and analogy of its resemblances and differences: craft indeed but founded on perceptions and laminations of the spirit so multitudinous and imperceptible, so buried under varieties of experience, that a hundred years of analysis would still leave the heart of the matter out.

Apart from this, I have watched Aeschylus closely. Sound for sound, almost syllable for syllable, I have tried to match the Master and create English equivalents for his caparisonings. I have plunged into his majesty and passion—and, be it confessed, into his grandiloquence; soaked myself in his richness. If I seem to emerge at times a little too spangled, some of it at least has come from my encounter.

Most translators, it is presumed, try to achieve maximum fidelity both to the letter and the spirit of the original: a difficult feat, since these by no means always agree. In my own efforts, my principles have been the following:

One language best translates another when it remains most true to itself. The genius of each must be respected, as an artist respects his medium and material. And no language can take a sonic photograph of another. In other words, English says most about Greek when it is most like English. Therefore, I have not tried to imitate, but to create equivalent impressions by transposing parallel patterns of sound.

The Greek of Aeschylus is magnificent and beautiful. Therefore, whenever I have found my fidelity to the letter producing something prosaic, awkward, and ugly, I have deemed myself guilty of essential mistranslation, and tried again. The Greek of Aeschylus is also both formal and free; creating an illusion of spontaneity even in the most weighted phrase. Therefore, when I have caught myself being merely stiff and heavy, I have tried again.[1]

Greek poetry can be strong and even harsh, but in

---

[1] Though there are times when Aeschylus himself is stiff and heavy.

general it is distinguished by "melopoeia"—a sweet-singing ease which makes it a delight to the ear. Therefore, I have tried to sing.

Aeschylus is rich in figures of speech and in all the phonic devices of language. He is incredibly rich in assonance, consonance, and alliteration. Therefore (like an old hen picking up a pebble), I have weighed every syllable of his for its vowels and consonants, sound and sense, before I have tried to balance it with something in English.

Aeschylus uses a surprising amount of rhyme and near-rhyme, though, since Greek is an inflected language, this is apt to go undetected. I too have used rhyme even though in English rhyme is far less unobtrusive.

The choruses of Aeschylus are close-packed, loaded, difficult. I have not tried to make them easy.

The dialogue of Greek tragedy is for the most part in iambic trimeter. Like the English hexameter it is a line of twelve syllables and six accents. But, curiously, the Greek trimeter is *not* the esthetic equivalent of the English hexameter, as I pointed out in my translations of Sophocles.[2] "The Greek trimeter is light and quick, the English hexameter dawdles and hesitates." I was taken to task by a certain critic for this, who said that I would have been more exact and more modest if I had looked around me first. Had I not seen the wonders produced by Messers X, Y, and Z in an English iambic "trimeter?" My answer, *salva reverentia,* is that these gentlemen have indeed produced a very interesting hexameter line, full of variety and full of movement, but still it succeeds only by default. Which is to say, that it succeeds only so long as one does not read it as hexameter. It breaks down into separate little knots of trimeter, tetrameter, dimeter—or whatever is necessary to get the line scanning. But once give the line its true prosodic value and the old difficulty remains: the line is too long for English dramatic poetry. It becomes "talky." The reason is simple: twelve syllables of English generally take several seconds longer to say

2 *The Oedipus Plays of Sophocles.* New York: The New American Library (Mentor Books), 1958.

than twelve syllables of Greek. It is not merely that the English vowels tend to be longer than the Greek but that English uses almost twice the number of consonants—and consonants delay. In epic poetry of course this does not matter; but in drama it does.[8]

The line which I have adopted is predominantly iambic, but variable in foot and meter. It can stretch to heptameters or shrink to dimeters: whatever is necessary—not to fill out the scanning, but to accommodate the dramatic emphasis and timing of living speech. It is a line which should always be given its full prosodic value in reading, because the feeling of the words is built into a definite measure. This is not hard for an actor to do, for the line, while keeping to a beat (as the Greek does), always follows the sense. The meter noses in after the sense and seldom militates against it—as it so often has to in traditional blank verse. If the actor will speak the lines as they are written, and not run them into one another, he will achieve the rhythm (perhaps even the meter) I intended, and so three quarters of the feeling.

When I have spoken to actors about the paramount necessity of reading according to the meter they have mistaken me to mean a singsong delivery with all the la-di-das of a twelve-year-old reciting. Nothing could be further from my intention. I should always hope to hear the natural voice with the natural stresses and all the dramatic underlining that is felt necessary. But the reader must be conscious of, and have previously mastered, the correct metrical pointing, allowing this to show up underneath as a counterpoint rhythm or syncopation. Not to do so is to remove from English dramatic poetry—and of course from the Greek—that unique tension of stress, rhythm, and sense which makes its cadence so interesting and so moving. A reader will know artistically that he has succeeded when he feels himself giving an impression of naturalness, ease, restraint, and right emphasis.

[8] The most splendid recent example, to my mind, of the English hexameter in epic is Mr. Kimon Friar's translation of Nikos Kazantzakis's *Odyssey: A Modern Sequel.* New York: Simon and Schuster, 1958.

The meter of the Greek choruses is very irregular. I have usually tried to follow it, but at a distance. The lyric meters in Greek are intricate indeed, and I have seldom seen them successfully copied in English. The reason in general is that:

> In Greek the style is simple and the grammar complex, while in our languages the style is comparatively complex and the grammar simple . . . it is wholly impossible to reproduce in any of our languages, particularly in English, the complicated grammatical structure of so highly syllabic and syntactic a language as Ancient Greek.[4]

Or to make the difference even more specific and prosodic:

> Greek metric is not accentual, but quantitative. That is to say, the rhythm is based on units in which the balance of syllables is dictated not by the loudness, or stress, with which it is spoken, but by quantity, or the time taken to speak it. Even so simple a form as the dactylic hexameter has a precision and a formality which is almost impossible in accentual verse; for no accent is quite strong enough to do what quantity can, and English hexameters too often limp and languish. . . . It is just possible to write English hexameters, and with some difficulty to produce Alcaics and Sapphics, but it is quite impossible to compose anything resembling the complex meters of Greek choral poetry like that of Pindar or the songs of the Tragedians and Aristophanes, for the simple reason that the English accent falls so dubiously and hesitantly that we can never quite know what the rhythm is, whereas in Greek it is perfectly clear and emphatic from the start.[5]

I have never tried to be clear at all costs. The relation of poetry to clarity is subtle indeed. There is something in poetry over and above the mere understanding of the

4 Arnold J. Toynbee (tr.). *Greek Historical Thought.* Boston: Beacon Press, 1950; New York: The New American Library (Mentor Books), 1952.
5 C. M. Bowra, *op. cit.*

words: a surprise, a movement, a rising off the ground, which it shares with music. Good poetry communicates immediately, long before the words are understood. It has been well said that obfuscation and woolliness have made plenty of bad poems, but mere clarity has never made a good one.

In each of the plays here represented I use a different typography. This is experimental and incidental. In a mobile adaptation of the iambic pentameter as a free-wheeling instrument designed to capture both formality and spontaneity, I have tried to see which best follows the rise, fall, and excitement of the human voice.

APPENDIX II

CLYTEMNESTRA AND IRONY

It has been well remarked (and I wish I could remember the source of the quotation) that: "Clytemnestra is one of the most powerful characters in history. Very little is said about her: she acts. And she never wavers. She is a Lady Macbeth who does *not* crumble at the end. Not quite human but altogether gloriously and grandly disreputable."

The modern reader might at first sight think it odd that she does not show more active signs of her double-dealing. How are we to know that she is not being sincere in her opening speech and in her further two speeches? Surely at their face value they do evince every sign of love and loyalty? Here we come to the crux of a Greek play—the whole difference between it and most of ours: the Greeks already knew the plot; we do not. This alters everything. Aeschylus has no need to build Clytemnestra up, or waste time giving external signs of her murderous intentions. For those who already know, *everything* is an external sign, and everything is innocent—as in real life a murderer might be indistinguishable from the rest. All that matters is that we see her words and actions in a double light.

APPENDIX III

THE THEOLOGY OF AESCHYLUS

We lack what may have been Aeschylus's most complete theological statement, contained in the two lost plays of the Promethean trilogy. In the *Prometheus Bound,* the only extant member, we have a repetition (or a first draft) of the Zeus in *The Agamemnon.* In both sets of plays the theological movement seems to have been parallel, and by analogy we can, I think, surmise the extent to which Aeschylus humanized and enlarged his concept of God.[1]

In *The Agamemnon* we have a Zeus still overly conscious of his own Titanic, barbaric past; still very much the Old Testament god of "an eye for an eye and a tooth for a tooth"; simple and vindictive. By the end of *The Eumenides* he has changed. The Furies, those goddesses of strict retributive justice who represented his powers of judging and punishing, have themselves been mellowed by the action of Apollo and Athena—also representatives of Zeus and standing for Enlightenment and Compassion. In other words, Zeus himself has evolved, and now embodies in himself the disparate attributes of the deities, summing them up in a trinity of Justice, Enlightenment, and Compassion. Only one thing remains: the union of Zeus with Fate. And *that* in the last triumphant shout of *The Eumenides* is accomplished:

Zeus the All-seeing and Fate

[1] In this context of natural theology I mean *God* and not *a god.*

Have come to terms at last.

Aeschylus, of course, does not speak as a Christian, but he does speak as a prophet, and he does speak with the voice of humanity. He leaves a testament both deifying and humanizing. He is not one simply to throw away the anthropomorphic polytheism of the pre-Christian Greeks. He enshrines and sublimates it, realizing an alchemy wherein even the too-small ideas man has of God can be fused into greatness. The real Zeus, the Zeus in whom all is reconciled, subsumes into his eternal activity the functions of all Apollos, all Athenas, all Furies. And by identifying himself with Fate, Necessity itself, he relates every human being in all his actions to the total movement of history. The divine is no longer abstract but concrete, and all men are seen to face the same infinite but splendid predicament.

> O Zeus the unknown god, if Zeus
> Be his best title, hail by that:
> Incomparable!
> Undivinable in style!
> Unmatched Zeus, my only hope
> Of shedding from my soul
> The inept weight of worry.[2]

Whatever it is the gods may mean, whatever range of activity or mode of essence, *that* exactly it is on which each human structure is founded. The vast facade of Zeus as Father of All is itself the eternal carapace beneath which each brick of reality is supported. Finite and infinite are no longer separate terms but coefficients and coterminals: the back to the front, the outer to the inner, the down to the up. There is no other dimension through which man attains his stature, for there can be no touch upon our humanity, whether of darkness or joy, pain or futility, which is not the touch of God:

[2] *The Agamemnon*: first Stasimon, Strophe 2.

He leads us on the way of wisdom's
Everlasting law that truth
Is only learnt by suffering it.
Ah! in sleep the pain distills,
Bleeding on the memory,
And makes us wise against our wills:
God's grace by solemn force.[3]

[3] *The Agamemnon*: first Stasimon, Strophe 3.

APPENDIX IV

AN INFORMAL
SURVEY OF THE GREEK THEATER

(1) What main features does a Greek play of the fifth century B.C. share with one of today?

Both are *plays*: a set of words to be spoken by actors which pretends to unfold certain events as well as the thoughts and feelings of two or more characters. Both portray (presumably) some kind of conflict; both can be either tragic or comic or mixed; both can be written in poetic form, though a modern play usually is not; both can use a chorus or equivalent chorus, though a Greek play always does and a modern play rarely; both can proceed by the method of myth and symbol to state ultimate ideas through the specific actions and thoughts of characters in a story. Finally, both—at least we hope so—set out to be some form of art: that is, to reconstruct in a medium which is not life, but in a way we can understand or regret or enjoy—and in a form that is esthetically pleasing—the inner and outer aspects of our human condition.

(2) What are some of the differences?

i) The Greek theater was very much more than a place of entertainment. In fifth-century Athens it was also the semiritualistic expression of the culture and religion of a whole people. The plays were presented at festivals of great civic importance, to a garlanded audience. There were seats of honor for ambassadors, and visitors came from all over Greece. Later, when theaters had sprung up in almost every town of importance in the Mediterranean, drama became detached from its community origins and surrendered to a spirit of professionalism (though the profession of actor was highly honored), but in the best period it was very much a citizen art produced for a citizen audience by citizen performers. The playwrights did not hope to earn their living by it (though later the state seems to have paid an honorarium to each of the contending poets). They wrote for love of their art and in hope of renown.

ii) The Greek theater was never a mirror of superficialities, a platform for social reform, an analysis of the burdens of the common man. It did not try to produce a naturalistic replica of life but an idealized, that is, heightened, representation of it. Consequently it needed a powerful, high-geared, and inspired art to put it over: in poetry, song, and spectacle.

iii) The subject matter of Greek drama was almost always taken from the well-known stories of the gods and the heroes; consequently the plots were known to the audience in advance. The thrill of anticipation, the gradual unfolding of inevitable disaster, took the place of suspense. Dramatic irony took the place of discovery. The Greek dramatist was free to concentrate his artistry on *how* a thing was done rather than on *what* was done. He did not have to include for the sake of information or realism the tedious and the banal. He could leave out a great deal and thereby intensify his emotive power.

iv) Greek drama depicted; modern drama displays. The genius of the one was to bring a scene to life by the power of words; of the other, by actual vision. In a Greek play erotic passion, physical violence, murder, were described verbally, never or rarely shown. The horror of the unseen—but imagined—took the place of the horror (all too easily the nausea) of the seen. In a modern play these things are shown visually rather than described: words tend to become secondary to what is done and actually visualized.[1] In the art of the cinema or television words might almost be said to have become redundant. Greek plays, on the contrary, consisted mainly of speeches and songs, separated by rapid passages of alternate line dialogue (stichomythia) made exciting by the cut and thrust of debate. The songs were musically accompanied, mimed and danced. The form, therefore, was by no means static, the content even less so. Precisely because the burden of having to reproduce a visual replica of action was avoided and the poet was free to create an illusion or idealization of reality, words took wing, crossed the seas, fought with armies, entered the boudoirs of queens, delved into the motives of murderers, discovered the aspirations of heroes. There was nothing to limit the range and power of the Greek playwright but his own imagination and his mastery of words.

v) Greek plays took place outside. Indoor scenes were either reported or revealed to the audience through the "ekkyklema," "something rolled out"—a kind of platform which was rolled out through the skene doors—though it is not impossible that interior scenes were also shown by the doors suddenly opening.

vi) Stage scenery was of the simplest sort or nonexistent, though its introduction has been ascribed to both Aeschylus and Sophocles. Tragedies were usually set before a temple or palace, comedies before a street of houses. The permanent architectural background could by the mere words and gestures of an actor become the seashore, a cave or a mountain. Besides the ekkyklema there were other stage devices, the most important of which was the "machine"—a kind of crane which could make gods appear and disappear or fly through the sky. There was no artificial lighting—though torches could be used for spectacular processional effects—and all scenes, even night, were acted in broad day. To sum up: in the greatest period of Greek drama the keynote

---

[1] I am, of course, describing the general trend, not the innumerable exceptions.

was economy of means and absolute reliance on the imaginative artistry of the spoken word.

vii) All parts were acted by male actors, of whom— since the time of Sophocles—there was a maximum of three. By changing his mask the same actor could take on two or more parts. There were, however, extras and supers: retinues for tragic kings and queens, soldiers, servants, and attendants.

viii) Since there was no proscenium curtain (and no need for one) plays were presented without break from start to finish—an enormous saving of cumulative dramatic power.

(3) Did the Greeks have a somewhat different idea of tragedy from us?

Here is Aristotle's famous definition of tragedy, drawn from, and formulated a hundred years after, the golden age of Greek drama: "Tragedy, then, is an imitation of an action that is serious, complete, and of a certain magnitude; in language embellished with every kind of artistic ornament, the several kinds being found in separate parts of the play; in the form of action, not of narrative;[2] through pity and fear effecting the proper purgation of these and similar emotions."[3]

(4) Would you say, then, that modern tragedy (dating it roughly from Ibsen, Strindberg, and Chekhov) is more pessimistic than Greek tragedy?

In the sense that Greek tragedy did not necessarily have to end unhappily, yes; or that even when it did so the mood and intention were to reinforce rather than to undermine man's belief in the value of living—again, yes. Curiously, however, it is we and not the Greeks who tend to believe in the perfectibility of man. Yet the tone of modern tragedy has been far more pessimistic. Many of our plays leave us with little more than a painstaking

[2] I.e., the story is acted, not merely told.
[3] *Poetics:* 1449b.

record of the slow attrition and disintegration of the human person. The manner, too, is far from sublime or encouraging. We have been tempted to doubt the validity of free will, hence of personal responsibility, hence of the hero. It follows that the grand manner is suspect too. A theater that centers precisely on the "common man," often the vicious man, dwells on insight rather than on illumination. We have produced a race of playwrights that speaks brilliantly for a generation lost and disillusioned. And yet, when all is said and done, murder, suicide, incest, adultery, war, or—if one puts it in terms of emotion—anger, revenge, despair, lust, pride, power—remain equally the raw material of Greek as of modern tragedy. It is the manner rather than the matter that has changed. And if one is tempted to think that the modern approach, with all its post-Freudian insight, gets nearer to the eternal verities and to the mind and heart of man, he has simply to put Jean Anouilh's *Antigone* next to Sophocles' for his answer. In the great tragedies of Aeschylus, Sophocles, and Euripides, the courage with which the whole human situation is challenged, and the sublimity to which it is raised by the universality of the thought and the beauty of the language, are themselves vehicles of hope, gratitude, and ennoblement.

(5) How did so noble an art arise?

This is largely a matter of guesswork and there are several rival theories. What is certain is that it grew slowly through several centuries and that it developed out of choral song. This song became the "dithyramb": a kind of mimic hymn-dance performed by fifty men dressed as satyrs and celebrating the deeds of the god Dionysus, who was the deity of luxuriant fertility, especially of the vine. In time (some scholars propose: from the beginning), the deeds of other gods and heroes also became the material for these sagas. There came into existence a body of narrative poetry essentially dramatic in content, though not in form. The moment one of the chorus stepped aside and began to converse with the rest as a priest-actor, a new art sprung from the dithyramb and drama was born. The move is traditionally ascribed to Thespis, who thus became "the Father of Drama." One other great step was necessary before tragedy could develop freely: the separation of the wildly fertility-minded satyric elements from the movement of serious drama—in other words, the invention of the satyr play. This step is said to have been taken by Pratinas, who wrote about 500 B.C. It was Aeschylus, according to Aristotle, who introduced a second actor[4] and thus initiated dramatic conflict in dialogue between two characters. He also reduced the size of the chorus from fifty to twelve and made it active in the drama; invented elaborate costuming and perhaps stage scenery and the painted mask; created new dances; and wrote the first great Greek plays that have come down to us. Under Aeschylus the choral lyric of early Greek drama turned into lyric tragedy: the dramatic lyric became lyric drama.

(6) You speak as though the two forms are distinct.

They are, but under Aeschylus they were fused into one: ". . . due partly to the historical accident in which two forms of fiction were combined: drama, still relatively primitive and naive, with choral lyric, now after generations of mature practice, brought to its highest point of development by Simonides and Pindar. But the direction taken by the form is due also to deliberate choice. The desire is to transcend the limitations of dramatic presentation, even before these limitations have been firmly established."[5]

(7) Do we know the names of any of the tragic poets before the coming of Aeschylus?

[4] Sophocles raised the number of actors to three and the number of the chorus to fifteen. According to Aristotle he introduced scene painting.
[5] Professor Richmond Lattimore, Introduction to his translation of the *Oresteia. Aeschylus. Complete Works.* 2 vols. ed. by David Grene and Richmond Lattimore. Vol. 1, *Oresteia.* Chicago: University of Chicago Press, 1953.

Yes, but not their works, or only fragments. Thespis, Pratinas, Choerilus, Phrynicus, had all made some kind of name for themselves before the coming of Aeschylus. Thespis (sixth century B.C.), by introducing an actor to play against the chorus, is regarded as the father of Greek drama. Besides bringing in dialogue he enlarged the subject matter of drama, though still apparently keeping it within the Dionysian cycle of myths. It was not till about 535 B.C. that tragedy was officially recognized by the Athenian state and given publicly sponsored contests and performances.

The most famous tragic poet before Aeschylus was Phrynichus. He won his first victory in 511 B.C. and won again in 476. He seems to have been the first to break away from stories revolving round the god Dionysus and to use Homer as an inexhaustible quarry. He introduced new measures and dances for the chorus and was styled "Master of all singers," whose songs were "sweet as the honey of a bee." Phrynicus also seems to have been the first to adapt contemporary events to drama. Two of his plays dealt with historical subjects, and in 494 B.C. he portrayed on the stage the capture of Miletus, which had just fallen to the Persians.

As to Choerilus of Athens, we know that he competed against Aeschylus in 499 B.C. and was at his height in 482. He seems to have been especially gifted in satyric drama, the invention of his younger contemporary, Pratinas.

A little later in the fifth century there was Ion, the popular writer and elegant stylist; the clever and facile Agathon—the first to write a drama on a subject not connected with mythology or history, whose choruses became musical interludes and whose style is said to have been florid. There were also Neophron of Sicyon, Aristarchus of Tegea, Archaeus of Eretria. They were all prolific writers, but by the unanimous consent of antiquity there was nobody to compare with the big four: Aeschylus, Sophocles, Euripides, and Aristophanes. The next important name is that of Menander, but that takes us into the fourth and third centuries B.C., when the greatest period of Greek drama was over.

(8) From where did the Greek dramatists of the fifth century draw their material?

Principally from the old stories of the gods and heroes as handed down by oral and written tradition in epic and lyric poetry, particularly from the *Iliad* and *Odyssey* of Homer. Homer became a kind of bible-*cum*-history of the ancient world, and a compendium of its values. Occasionally a drama was built upon contemporary history, as in *The Persians* of Aeschylus—the story of the repulse by the Greeks of the mighty army of Xerxes—but in general the Greek dramatists did not depart from their sources of epic legend. Within these limits they felt free to select, expand, reshape and interpret, drawing from them new developments of theme, plot, and character. For example, Aeschylus, Sophocles, and Euripides all wrote plays on the Oedipus cycle, though only those of Sophocles have survived.

(9) You said that the Greek theater was much more than a place of entertainment. In what way?

It never quite lost its religious motive and impetus. Even apart from its liturgical origins—hymns and dances around the altar of Dionysus [6]—Greek drama was imbued with a powerful moral and ethical sense which sought not only to inspire but to teach. The plays of the three great tragic poets—and even of the comic playwright, Aristophanes—are profoundly theological. Man's ways with God or the gods—and vice versa—are explored throughout, side by side with the ever-important and always bewildering questions of destiny, freedom, personal responsibility, and sin, especially the sin of pretension and overweening self-assertion (*hybris*). Within such an anthropotheological framework are also pre-

[6] Which became forever afterward the pivotal point in the orchestra and was called the "thymele."

sented man's ways with man: honor, justice, retribution, law, liberty, duty; and his universal emotions: love, hate, revenge, fear, pride, pity, and regret. These are the themes and emotions which pulse through the stories taken by the Greek poets from their heroic past and turned by them into dramas of surpassing power, significance, and beauty.

(10) Was the Greek theater popular?

Enormously. When the young Aeschylus first came into dramatic conflict with his celebrated contemporaries, Pratinas and Choerilus, in 499, it drew such crowds that the wooden scaffolding on which the spectators sat collapsed (which led to the Athenians building their first stone theater). But even apart from the intrinsic fascination of the plays themselves, it was the right and duty of citizens to attend.

(11) When were the chief Athenian dramatic festivals?

The three most important were held every year in midwinter and spring. They were the City Dionysia (or Great Dionysia) in March/April, the Rural Dionysia in December/January, and the Lenaea in January/February. The first of these was devoted mainly to tragedy, and the third to comedy. The City Dionysia opened with two days of processions, pageantry, hymns and dances in honor of Dionysus. The last three days were taken up entirely with drama. The three tragic poets competing each furnished a set of three tragedies and a mock-heroic pastoral called a "satyr play." These sets of four plays, tetralogies, could either elaborate on a single theme or be a collection of plays each on a different subject. Each poet was allowed a team of three (at first, two) actors and a chorus of twelve or (after Sophocles) fifteen, as well as supernumeraries. There also competed five (in wartime three) comic poets, offering a play apiece. They were allowed the same number of actors but a chorus of twenty-four. In both tragedies and comedies the poets wrote not only their plays but the music and

choreography to go with them. They also directed, saw
to the costumes and scenery, and, at least till the time of
Sophocles, acted. Sophocles seems to have been the first
to discontinue this practice, considering his voice not
strong enough.

(12) Who financed these proceedings?

The city shared expenses with some wealthy member
of the community who was specially selected for each
playwright and known as the "choregus." The authority
who governed the whole festival was the "archon," and
any poet wishing to compete submitted to him his plays
for reading. If the plays were accepted the poet was
"granted a chorus." Then it was the choregus who paid
for the training and equipping of that chorus. The state
paid for the actors. The winning poet was crowned with a
wreath in the presence of the multitude, a distinction
that made him one of the most important members of the
nation. There were prizes of wreaths also for the star
actor and the choregus, who was allowed to erect a
monument in honor of his victory.

(13) How many people could a theater hold?

Probably between fourteen and twenty thousand,
but there seems to be a surprising divergence of opinion. One modern authority gives the seating capacity of
the theater at Epidaurus as seventeen thousand, of the
theater at Megalopolis as nineteen thousand, and of the
theater of Dionysus at Athens as fourteen thousand. However, we do not know what extra standing capacity
there may have been. Plato speaks of a play of Agathon
having been witnessed by thirty thousand in the same
theater of Dionysus.

(14) What kind of people went to the theater?

Every kind, including children and probably slaves.[7]

---

[7] It must be remembered that the Athenian slave could be and often
was a highly educated person.

It was by no means a highbrow, though it seems to have been a sensitive and lively, audience. There are plenty of stories of spectators being moved to tears or anger, or made wild with anticipation. In the fourth century and afterward, when the Greek theater had reached its peak and the interest of the audience had largely shifted from the poets to the actors, ". . . both Plato and Aristotle speak of poets and actors lowering themselves to suit the depraved taste of a public dominated by the less cultivated elements in it." [8] But at least in the fifth century, the century of Aeschylus, Sophocles, and Euripides, ". . . our general conclusion must be that an audience which could follow devotedly the three great tragedians day after day, and could enjoy the wit of Aristophanes, must have possessed on the whole a high degree of seriousness and intelligence, and though there was always a possibility of lower elements gaining the upper hand for a moment, the great poets . . . never played down to them." [9]

It should be said in passing that women of the higher classes usually stayed away from the comedies and satyr plays. These never quite lost their nexus with the old fertility rites and motives. They were phallic, farcical, and frankly indecent, an outlet for animal spirits. The costumes were grotesque and obscenely padded. And one can guess what gestures no doubt went with them.

(15) How could the actors be heard in such vast theaters in the open air?

The acoustics of these theaters (as can still be tested) were amazingly good. In the large theater at Epidaurus, for instance, a clear but not over-loud conversation on the actors' platform can be heard in the uppermost ring of seats. Moreover, the Greeks spent a great deal of time on music and voice production. One might almost say

---

8 Sir Arthur Pickard-Cambridge, *The Dramatic Festivals of Athens,* to which I am indebted throughout. Oxford: The Clarendon Press; New York: Oxford University Press, 1953.
9 *Ibid.*

that the whole of Greek drama, from the first line composed by the poet to the last ode sung by the chorus, was a question of sound: inventing the right sounds in words and music; keeping them under trembling control so that as they hit the ear they seeped into the human heart and there, slowly and unobtrusively, delineated and refined the central passion. It was by the sound of his words as much as by the excellence of his drama— their power and aptness—that a poet moved his audience and so was judged. It was by the delicacy and beauty with which an actor was able to manipulate those sounds that he won his popularity. Voice production was the most important of all the theatrical properties. There is plenty of evidence that actors trained themselves rigorously, fasting and dieting and testing their voices repeatedly before performances and during intervals, to discipline them and bring them into condition.

(16) Was drama spoken or sung?

The dialogue was almost certainly spoken, though there may well have been background music to it. The choral parts, except where the chorus leader joins in the nonlyric dialogue, were sung or chanted.

(17) Do we know anything about the music?

Flutes, drums, cymbals, and trumpets were used, and perhaps occasionally the lyre. However, we know very little about the quality of Greek music, since our knowledge of it (except for a single fragment) begins two hundred years after the time when choral odes were an essential part of drama. There can be no doubt that though the music was important, musical accompaniment was strictly subordinate to the words. "Let the flute follow the dancing revel of the song—it is but an attendant." (Pratinas of Phlius, the great exponent of satyric drama, writing early in the fifth century B.C.)

(18) Is it true that the acting was statuesque and stylized, and that the costumes were grotesque?

It is true that in tragedy the acting was formal, restrained, and seldom violent; but that it was statuesque in the sense of wooden or monolithic is certainly an exaggeration. Though the Greeks were not aiming at realism or naturalism, they *were* aiming at a heightened effect of the real and the natural, something which any kind of excess—especially of the grand manner—would certainly kill. As to the costuming, if one excludes the satyr plays, it was not until a later and decadent period that the grotesque became popular. In its golden age the blend of formality and realism in the Greek theater would hardly have seemed more statuesque to us than grand opera does, or the miming, say, of a Marcel Marceau or a Jean Louis Barrault.

(19) How were the actors able to express their feelings through masks?

The mask stylized the predominant features of a character. Since the characters in a Greek play were not "round," but showed more or less one face to the world, masks could be appropriate and convincing, especially as in such vast theaters personal changes of feature would largely have gone unseen. As to other ways of depicting character, the Greek actor was free to display his feelings through an almost limitless range of gesture, which the Athenians considered of paramount importance: slow and fast movements, kneeling, leaping, lying, turning. If there occurred a momentary discrepancy between what an actor felt and what his mask expressed —some sudden access of grief or joy—he could always hide this by making a movement: turning, embracing, stooping. There must have been changes of mask too: in *Oedipus the King,* for instance, after Oedipus has blinded himself, and in *Hecuba* after the blinding of Polymnestor.

(20) Did the members of the chorus wear masks too?

Probably, and identical masks, though this was by no means always so. In *The Birds* of Aristophanes, for instance, many kinds of birds are represented. When it comes to human types and categories such as age, youth, citizenship, slavery—for example, the Old Men of *The Agamemnon,* the Young Captive Women of *The Eumenides,* the Citizens of Thebes in the *Oedipus Rex*—each would be depicted in different and appropriate masks.

(21) What about the "cothurnos" or thick-soled, high-padded shoes the actors were supposed to have worn?

Scholars differ. Some say that they were among the innovations designed by Aeschylus; others, that they came in only at a later and decadent period. Here is Sir Arthur Pickard-Cambridge: "The theory that actors wore shoes in which the thickness of the soles was increased to four and even eight or ten inches is no longer supported by any scholar of reputation." [10] (But he is referring only to the fifth century B.C.)

(22) What was the composition of the chorus?

Originally the chorus numbered fifty. It was cut down to twelve by Aeschylus,[11] raised to fifteen by Sophocles, and was twenty-four in the satyr plays and comedies of Aristophanes.

The chorus entered the stage to march music and grouped itself in the "orchestra" in a rectangular formation presenting a block of three files and five ranks,[12] with a front of three members, thus:

1	6	11
2	7	12
3	8	13
4	9	14
5	10	15

[10] *Op. cit.*

[11] Though he may occasionally have gone back to the larger number, as is thought possible in *The Eumenides.*

[12] "Weaker performers were kept in the middle, where they would be less obvious. Thus 'middle row of the chorus' had the derogatory sense which 'back row' had in our musical comedies." From Peter D. Arnott, *An Introduction to the Greek Theatre.* New York: The Macmillan Company, 1961. By far the soundest and most informative popular exposition I have come upon.

The dances had a military precision to them, with stately shiftings of the body, ordered gestures, and scant locomotion. The chorus's entries and departures were preceded by the flute player, who might be richly dressed. The entry of the chorus in *The Agamemnon*, with its anapaestic marching measure, is a typical entry of one of the earlier plays. The last fourteen lines of *The Eumenides* are a typical finale. In those plays which have no anapaestic opening for the chorus (*Antigone, Oedipus Rex, Hippolytus, Iphigeneia in Aulis,* and others), the chorus entered perhaps singing the strophes and antistrophes of the parodos (first ode), though it might equally well have entered mute, with the flutist playing a prelude. After that the members of the chorus would take up their positions and face the audience to sing.[13]

(23) What was the function of the chorus?

In the early days of Greek drama, when it was little more than a choral epic with lyric sequences sung by fifty performers, the chorus took almost no part in the action. Later, the occasional dialogue between it and the one actor was simply an interlude in the choric dance. Later still, under Aeschylus, with a chorus cut down to twelve and with two actors, it began to enter the dramatic action itself.

Under Sophocles the chorus retained its importance, but more as an intermediary between the actors (now three) and the audience. It answered the need for someone to represent the "man in the street," who could comment, give information, sum up, and, on occasion, set forth the poet's own views and feelings. In general, the function of the chorus became to underline the action of the plot, comment on the characters, bring out and unify the emotional and moral implications of the story, give relief from tension, and, finally, by its unique means

13 It must be remembered that there was no proscenium curtain.

of dance, song, and high-powered poetry, double the emotional involvement of the audience.

All these properties remained true of the chorus under Euripides, but less so. With his modern vision focused on the psychology of men and women themselves, the comments of the chorus, whether in dialogue or ode, began to become unnecessary. The choral songs (in their first step toward disappearing altogether) became interludes rather than contributions to the drama.

(24) Did the chorus speak or only sing?

Those parts where the coryphaios (leader of the chorus) joined in the nonlyric dialogue were certainly spoken. At other times (a notable example would be the huddle of old men immediately after the murder of Agamemnon) several members of the chorus spoke individually. As to the odes of the parodos and stasima, these were sung or chanted by the whole chorus in unison. Infinite pains must have been taken with the clear and evocative enunciation of the words. There are no grounds for thinking that the chorus ever *spoke* in unison. All speaking was done either by the chorus leader or by single members.

(25) Do the strophes and antistrophes correspond to a division of the chorus into two semichoruses which answered each other?

This was certainly true of some of the choruses of Aristophanes. As to the other playwrights, scholars differ. Sir Arthur Pickard-Cambridge says there is no evidence for this. On the other hand, it is difficult to see a reason for strophe and antistrophe if some such arrangement did not obtain, although strophe, which means turning, and antistrophe, turning back, could have referred to the pivotal movements of the whole chorus. Beyond this there is no reason to suppose that the chorus repeated its actions in strophe and antistrophe (different words always call for different gestures), though the music probably *was* repeated. As to the events in the play, the members of the chorus must have suited their actions to the drama not only when they were singing the odes but throughout the speeches and movements of the main characters.

(26) Do we know anything about the dances of the Greek chorus?

Little for certain, except that they were stately and restrained and not what we ordinarily mean by "dancing." Music and the dance, however, were considered by the Athenians as the keystones of education. One could not have a healthy mind in a healthy body if that body was dumb to music and movement. Sophocles himself was an accomplished dancer, and as a lad of sixteen danced before the trophy after the Greek victory at Salamis, playing the lyre. He also joined in the girls' ball game on the beach in his own tragedy of *Nausicaa*. We know too that the dance was chiefly mimetic: symbolizing character, emotion, and action through gesture and rhythmic movement. Great use was made of the hands, and of the movements of the body—bending, stooping, turning, swaying—which could express feeling without necessarily any locomotion at all.[14] Peter Arnott, describing a modern production of a Greek tragedy at Epidaurus, writes:

The chorus movements are directed with great beauty and skill. Now advancing on the audience, now retreating, now crossing the orchestra in a diagonal pattern, now draping themselves frieze-like along the front of the stage, they maintain an unbroken formal unity against which the action proceeds. Their movements echo and emphasize the emotions expressed on the stage. They cower at moments of fear, raise their arms aloft in triumph, swirl apart and come together in excitement. The chorus is used not only to deliver its own part but as a constant balletic accompaniment of the actors.[15]

14 At a later period in Greek history, pantomimic dancing became the most popular form of entertainment.
15 *Op. cit.*

This description, I believe, would essentially fit a tragic chorus of fifth-century Athens.

(27) Was admission to the theater free?

Admission was free at first; later by ticket. In the time of Demosthenes (fourth century B.C.) a seat cost 2 obols a day (equivalent to 25 cents or 1/6d). Since it was a civic duty to attend the festivals Pericles established a theater fund (the Theoric Fund) from which the poor citizens were given money to buy tickets. A great many of these tickets or tokens have been unearthed, ranging from the end of the fifth century B.C. until well on into the early Christian era. They look rather like coins and are of bronze, lead, ivory, bone, and terra cotta. There were special seats for distinguished persons (as usual, in the most conspicuous and least satisfactory places). It is probable that men and women sat in different parts of the auditorium, and that courtesans sat away from the other women.

(28) At what time of day did the plays begin?

At dawn. The dramatic poet for the day furnished a tetralogy of three tragedies and a satyr play. Finally the day ended with the performance of a comedy by one of the competing comic poets. Since the average time for a tragedy would be about an hour and three-quarters, a satyr play fifty minutes, and a comedy about an hour and fifty minutes, the total time needed for performances would be in the region of between seven and eight hours.

(29) This speaks of a patient and devoted audience!

Not always patient; devoted, yes—or should we say "passionately interested"? They flocked in from other states and towns, and from all over the countryside. The general air at the Great Dionysia or at the Lenaea must have been one of gaiety, expectation, and fiesta, with shops and booths erected everywhere. Many people probably brought their food with them and ate in the theater itself during intervals. Aristotle tells us that they did not even wait for the intervals if the acting was bad. Refreshments were peddled and sold in the theater, and there was time to go home to eat or rest between plays.

(30) How did the spectators endure those hard stone seats?

They brought mats, blankets, pillows. Distinguished guests and patrons were given their own cushions. There seem to have been awnings (at least at a later period) to shelter the two front rows from the sun—which in any case would not be excessive in January and March.

(31) You said the Greek audience was not always patient?

Nor did it try to hide its feelings. There is plenty of evidence of its noisiness both in approval and disapproval. Sometimes the poets themselves received punishment from their audience for real or imagined shortcomings. When Phrynichus brought to the stage the enactment of the recent fall of Miletus to the Persians, the Athenians burst into tears. Then (in typical Greek fashion), they fined him a thousand drachma (about $280 or £100) and forbade him ever to reproduce the drama. On another occasion, Aeschylus, acting in his own play and reciting lines about the goddess Demeter, was physically attacked by his audience, which had decided he was divulging secrets from the Eleusinian mysteries. The Athenians became so enraged that they rushed the stage, and the poet only escaped by taking sanctuary at one of the altars.[16] Later he was brought to trial—and acquitted. At other times actors or poets were forced to retire by the virulence of the audience's hissing, supplemented by the kicking of heels against the seats (which would have made a loud commotion in the days of the wooden seating). On the other hand the

16 The thymele in the center of the orchestra, or the altar in front of the skene.

audience was quick to show its approval too, and there is evidence that certain playwrights were not above currying favor with it. Menander—the great comic poet of the fourth and third centuries B.C.—once remarked to Philemon (a lesser writer who, nevertheless, had managed to defeat him several times through graft and bribery): "Tell me, Philemon, with absolute frankness: when you beat me don't you blush?"

(32) Do we know which plays of the great dramatists won first prize, and against whom?

In many instances, yes; just as we know a great many of the titles in the vast lost treasury of Greek plays. Aeschylus is reputed to have written some 90 plays, of which we have the titles of more than 80 and the fragments of over 70.[17] He was a success in his lifetime and won first prize thirteen times. Since on each occasion the poet entered four plays and was judged on the set, this means that Aeschylus entered the contest about twenty-two times. Thirteen victories in only twenty-two entries is certainly high success. He had been reigning some twenty-five to thirty years (assuming that the traditional dates are correct, and also that he would not have had four plays ready every single year) when he was defeated by the young Sophocles. However, he went on to win again next year with his *Seven Against Thebes*. The last time he won, before going off to the court of King Hieron of Syracuse where he died, was with the *Oresteia*.

Sophocles wrote some 123 plays, of which only seven have come down to us. He was a success with the Athenians from start to finish of his career and won 24 times, i.e., more often than Aeschylus and Euripides put together. He pleased the Athenians by giving an impression of restraint and unassailable orthodoxy, and while no less powerful than Aeschylus (who could frighten with his thunderous grandiloquence) he was both more natural and more suggestive. It is interesting

[17] But the complete texts of only seven.

to note, however, that he did not win with his greatest extant masterpiece, the *Oedipus Tyrannus,* which was defeated by Philocles, a nephew of Aeschylus.

Euripides, sixteen years younger than Sophocles but dying a year or two before him, seems to have been too psychological and too modern for the fifth-century audience, although in the century after his death he eclipsed his two great rivals in popularity. During his life he won the prize only four times. Of his reputed 90 plays we have 19. Euripides went into voluntary exile toward the end of his life, discouraged, no doubt, by the indifference of the Athenians to his tragedies. After his death in Macedonia at the court of King Archelaus, the Athenians, suddenly aware of what they had lost, gave him the prize for the fifth time.

Aristophanes wrote some 40 plays, of which we have only 11. He won only four first prizes and it is surprising that *The Birds*—perhaps his greatest masterpiece—was placed only second.

(33) Who judged in these dramatic contests?

The judges and their verdicts were arrived at by a complicated combination of election and lot drawing.

(34) Were the plays put on only three times a year and only at Athens?

These were the chief times, but there were others and at other places,[18] especially by the end of the fifth century B.C. Theaters sprang up throughout the Greek world, which had spread in its colonies all over the Mediterranean. After the death of Alexander the Great in 323 B.C. Hellenic culture extended even to the frontiers of India. Actors' guilds began to flourish and touring companies gave performances everywhere on fitted-up stages. Under Alexander, too, the custom had begun of celebrating all festivals with drama. "It is evident,"

---

[18] But of native drama in other parts of Greece we know very little.

writes Sir Arthur Pickard-Cambridge, "that the drama and music thus circulating throughout the Greek world was the most popular and influential form of culture for several hundred years."[19]

Nor must it be forgotten that besides the set times and places for the exhibition of drama in the fifth century B.C. the poets themselves gave readings of their plays. Indeed, in the ancient world a reading [20] to a select audience was the accepted form of publication. Manuscripts were copied, sold, read, and quoted. Also, plays could be, and were, put on more than once and in more than one place. Aeschylus, for instance, twice visited Sicily and produced his plays in the great theater at Syracuse. After his death the Athenians honored his memory with a decree which granted state backing to anyone who wanted to produce his plays. They were indeed produced (as were those of Sophocles and Euripides—posthumously) and Aeschylus, dead, won still more prizes over living poets.

(35) What happened to the Greek theater after the fifth century B.C.?

It went into a decline. Though there were descendants of both Aeschylus and Sophocles who continued to achieve a certain fame as playwrights, there were no more great tragic poets after the death of Sophocles in 405 B.C. And comedy, too, passed its peak in the life of Aristophanes himself (450–c.385). The only considerable playwright between the fourth and third centuries was Menander. Otherwise, in the post-Alexandrian period (and even before), the significant dramas performed throughout the Hellenistic world were revivals, and chiefly of Euripides (who thus more than redressed his balance with his two great rivals). It is ironic to think that Greek culture never spread so far or so fast as after the fall of Athens. And it went on spreading for

---

[19] *Op. cit.*
[20] There is a legend that Sophocles (at the age of ninety) hastened his death by giving a reading of the *Antigone*.

several hundred years—long after her miraculous period in art and literature was over. As to drama, it achieved a kind of fertile mediocrity. Tragedies became dull, conventional, and declamatory. Star performers took the place of star poets, and rhetoric became more important than poetry. Plays degenerated into "chamber drama" in that the quality of writing was more fitted for private reading than for public performance. When Alexandria, rich and new, became a center of culture in the third century B.C., drama did indeed have a final fling, but there is little or no record of its products. As far as we can tell, it seems to have been little more than a sophisticated scholarship exercising itself—self-consciously—in undramatic techniques.

(36) In producing or directing Greek tragedy what should be one's endeavor?

To create a unity of form and content so sublime yet so immediate that its very effulgence moves people to wonder, apprehension, sympathy, and tears. Every other consideration—authenticity of historical setting and theatrical convention—should be obliterated before the naked impact of idealized but essential human beings playing out the eternal emotions of mankind. Therefore, there must be art without artiness, dignity without aloofness, humanity without familiarity, the natural without naturalism. Finally, the total expression, in sound and sight, must glitter with color, pace, simplicity, and conviction: that is, *be beautiful.*

GLOSSARY OF NAMES AND PLACES

ACHAEA a province in the Peloponnesus; it later became a name for Greece and the Greeks.

ACHERON a river of the Underworld, the "river of eternal woe," across which Charon ferried the souls of the dead. Sometimes synonymous with Hades.

AEGEUS a king and hero of Athens, the father of Theseus. He killed himself when he thought Theseus was dead.

AEGYPLANCTUS a mountain in northern Greece.

AIDONEUS another name for Hades, god of the Underworld and brother of Zeus. The Underworld itself became known as Hades.

ALCMENE mother of Heracles (Hercules) by Zeus, who seduced her by taking the form of her husband Amphitryon.

ALTHEA the daughter of Thestius, king of Aetolia. When her son Meleager (later famed for slaying a ferocious boar) was a week old the Fates told her that he would die when the log in the hearth had burnt out. She immediately quenched it and put it away in a chest. However, when Meleager grew to manhood and one day quarreled with and slew his brothers (or uncles), Althea took out the firebrand again and threw it into the fire. When it had burnt to nothing Meleager was dead. In remorse she killed herself.

AMAZONS warlike women who were supposed to have

lived in Scythia near the Black Sea. Poets and artists delighted to represent them as stalwart fighters against the heroes.

APHRODITE goddess of love, the Roman Venus. She was the wife of Hephaestus (Vulcan), god of fire and forge, but her great and famous love was Adonis.

APOLLO son of Zeus and Leto. He was the god of music, prophecy, help and healing, reward and punishment, and had more influence upon the Greeks than almost any other single god. He came to be identified with Helios, god of the sun.

ARACHNUS "Spider's Mountain": a peak in the Peloponnesus.

ARES god of war: the Roman Mars; son of Zeus and Hera.

ARIA a district in Persia (Iran).

ARGOS a city-state in the eastern Peloponnesus and capital of ancient Argolis. The citizens were called "Argives."

ARTEMIS the Roman Diana: twin sister of Apollo and goddess of the moon, wild animals, and the hunt. She sent plagues and sudden death (especially to women) but she also cured and alleviated sufferings. She was also the goddess of virginity.

ASOPUS a river god and minor deity.

ATE goddess of evil, personifying reckless ambition and charged with bringing disgrace to man. She was a daughter of Zeus and a sister of the Furies.

ATHENA the Roman Minerva. Daughter of Zeus and Metis. Zeus swallowed her mother before her birth and Athena sprang from his head, fully armed and shouting a war cry. She was the goddess of power and wisdom, maintainer of law and order. She created the olive tree, invented the plow, and was adopted by the Athenians as their patroness.

ATHOS mountain in northeastern Greece.

ATREIDAE sons of Atreus—Agamemnon and Menelaus. Though Aeschylus makes them princes of Argos, they were in fact princes of the neighboring city of Mycenae, from which they were driven by their uncle Thyestes after he had killed Atreus. While in exile at the court of King Tyndareus of Sparta, Agamemnon, the elder brother, marries his daughter Clytemnestra, and reconquers Mycenae. Menelaus marries Helen and inherits the kingdom of Sparta.

ATTICA a division of Greece of which Athens was the principal city. It reached the height of its power in the fifth century B.C.

AULIS a harbor in Greece where the Greek armada assembled and lay for months before its attack on Troy.

BACCHANTS the celebrators of the religious revelry centered upon the god of wine and virescent growth, Dionysus (Bacchus).

CALCHAS soothsayer and priest of Apollo. He accompanied the Greek armies to Troy and told Agamemnon that he must sacrifice his daughter Iphigenia in order to win favorable winds for the Greek armada.

CASSANDRA daughter of Priam; she was endowed with the gift of prophecy, but to it was attached the curse that no one should ever believe her.

CHALCIS a town and peninsula in northeastern Greece.

CISSIA a district of Susiana, in which the city of Susa (capital of Persia) was situated.

CITHERON a mountain range separating Boeotia from Megaris and Attica.

COCYTUS river of "weeping and wailing" in the Underworld. A tributary stream of the Acheron.

CORYCIS a rock in Parnassus known also as the Nymphs' Cavern.

CRANAUS the mythical founder of the "rocky city," i.e., Athens.

CRETAN of the island of Crete in the southern Mediterranean where civilization seems to have dawned hundreds of years before it came to Greece.

CRONUS the Roman Saturn; youngest of the Titans and son of Uranus and Gaea (Heaven and Earth). He ousted his father from divine supremacy and was in his turn ousted by his son Zeus.

DANAIAN another name for the Greeks.

DAULIA an ancient town in Phocis, central Greece, on the gulf of Corinth.

DELOS smallest of the Cyclades islands. Birthplace of Apollo and Artemis; famous for its shrine of Apollo.

DELPHI a small town in Phocis; one of the most celebrated in all Greece because of its oracle of Apollo.

DELPHUS an early hero and son of Poseidon. He gave his name to the oracle at Delphi.

ERECHTHEUS a mythical king of Athens, said to be the son of Hephaestus and reared by Athena. He brought the cult of Athena to Athens. He gave his name to the Erechtheum, a famous temple on the Acropolis.

ERINYES the Furies, originally three in number, and daughters of Earth and darkness. They were the attendants of Hades and lived at the entrance of the Underworld. Their duty was punitive and purgative: to make criminals arriving at the shades expiate their crimes, and to harry the consciences of those who sinned. They were represented as pursuing with speed and fury, snakes writhing in their hair.

EURIPUS a channel between the island of Euboea and Boeotia in Greece. It was noted for the violent and unpredictable currents flowing in both directions.

FURIES the Erinyes, originally three: Tisiphone, Alecto, and Megaera.

GERYON a three-headed, three-bodied giant equipped with wings, lord of immense herds of cattle. Hercules killed him so that he could steal his cattle and so complete one of his twelve labors.

GORGONS three terrible sisters with snakes for hair; the mere sight of them turned people to stone. The most famous of them, Medusa, was slain by Perseus, who turned away his eyes and used his shield as a mirror.

GORGOPIS a bay in the Corinthian Gulf.

HADES the Roman Pluto; god of the Underworld (to which he gave his name) and brother of Zeus.

HELEN the most beautiful of women. She was the daughter of Zeus and Leda (whom Zeus seduced by turning himself into a swan) and the half-sister of Clytemnestra. She married Menelaus, brother of Agamemnon, and ran away to Troy with Paris, one of the fifty sons of King Priam. This was the abduction which began the Trojan War.

HELLAS originally a town in northeastern Greece. It became another name for the whole of Greece.

HEPHAESTUS the Roman Vulcan, god of the fire and forge, who fashioned Achilles' famous shield. He was the son of Zeus and Hera.

HERA the Roman Juno; official wife of Zeus and queen of the gods. She was the divine personification of feminine powers and the patroness of women.

HERMES the Roman Mercury, patron of guile and eloquence and the messenger of the gods. He is usually depicted as wearing winged shoes and hat and carrying the caduceus (winged stick entwined with serpents) in his hand. It was he who conducted the shades of the dead from the upper to the lower world.

IDA a mountain near Troy in Asia Minor.

ILIUM another name for Troy.

INACHUS a river-god and founder of Argos. He was the father of Io, whom Zeus loved and Hera changed into a cow.

IPHIGENIA daughter of Clytemnestra and Agamemnon. Her father sacrificed her at the altar to ensure favorable winds for the Greek fleet sailing against Troy.

IXION a king of Thessaly and father of the Centaurs. Zeus punished him for trying to seduce Hera and had him bound to a revolving wheel in Hades.

JUPITER Roman name for Zeus: father of the gods and ruler of Olympus.

LEDA mother of Helen and Pollux, by Zeus, and of Clytemnestra and Castor by her husband, Tyndareus.

LEMNOS an island in the Aegean where Hephaestus is supposed to have fallen to earth when Zeus (or perhaps his mother Hera) threw him out of heaven in a fit of annoyance. The LEMNIAN horror refers to the story that the women of Lemnos, angry with their husbands for keeping Thracian concubines, rose up against their men and killed them. When the Argonauts visited the island they found only women.

LETO mother of Apollo and Artemis. She fled to the island of Delos to escape the jealousy of Hera, and there gave birth to the twins.

LIBYA a country in North Africa (probably a coastal Greek colony settled by Athenians), where the inhabitants worshiped Athena.

LOXIAS another name for Apollo, especially under the formality of prophet.

LYCIA a small district in southern Asia Minor where Apollo was worshiped.

MACISTUS a mountain in Euboea: island in the Aegean.

MAIA the eldest and most beautiful of the Pleiades; the seven daughters of Atlas and Pleione whom Zeus placed among the stars. She was the mother of Hermes by Zeus but came to be confused with Maia the consort of Vulcan, who had her feast day on May 1.

MARS the Roman name for Ares, god of war.

MENELAUS king of Sparta, brother of Agamemnon, and husband of Helen.

MERCURY the Roman name for Hermes, messenger of the gods.

MESAPION town on the coast of Boeotia.

MINOS a wise and just king of Crete. He was the son of Europa, sired by Zeus in the form of a bull, who carried her all the way to Crete on his back. It was his grandson, Minos, for whom Daedalus constructed the labyrinth to house the Minotaur. The first Minos when he died became one of the judges of the Underworld.

MOIRA a general name for Fate, which godhead was divided into three persons: Clotho, Lachesis, and Atropos, representing birth, years, and death. They were outside the authority of Zeus and spun people's lives out of gold, silver, or wool, tightening and slackening the thread and at last snipping it off.

NISUS brother of Ageus, whom he assisted in recover-
ing the kingdom of Attica.

ODYSSEUS the Roman Ulysses, king of Ithaca, one of
the Ionian islands off the west coast of Greece. He
joined the Trojan War against his will, as an ally
of Agamemnon, and so began his legendary wan-
derings.

OLYMPUS the highest range of mountains separating
Macedonia and Thessaly. It was the seat of Zeus
and all his dynasty of gods and goddesses.

OURANOS or URANUS: a personification of Heaven. He was
the son of Gaea or Ge and by her the father of the
Titans, the Cyclopes and the Giants. Because he in-
sisted on concealing his children in the depths of the
earth, their mother stirred them up against him, and
finally Cronus, the youngest of the Titans, unseated
him with a sickle.

PAEAN the Healer; name for Apollo. Hence also a hymn
of thanksgiving to the gods, especially to Apollo.

PALLAS agnomen of Athena, goddess of wisdom.

PAN the Roman Faunus, god of shepherds, flocks, wild
animals, and woods and meadows. A lover of music
who invented the syrinx or shepherd's pipes, he led
the nymphs in dance and revelry. He also had a
reputation for lechery and was represented with the
legs and horns of a goat. Later the satyrs were confused with him: woodland deities who attended
Bacchus. Pan was said to be the son of a nymph
by Hermes (sometimes Zeus).

PARIS also called Alexander. He was one of the fifty
sons of Priam, king of Troy, and was raised as a
shepherd on Mount Ida (where he had been ex-
posed because his sister Cassandra had prophesied
that he would grow up to be the ruin of his country). Later, however, he returned to Troy as prince
and brought with him Helen the beautiful wife of

Menelaus, thus making himself the prime cause of the Trojan War. He killed Achilles by shooting him in the heel (his one vulnerable spot) and was himself killed by an arrow from the bow of Philoctetes.

PARNASSUS a mountain range in southern Greece overlooking Delphi. It was sacred to Apollo and the Muses, and also a seat of Dionysus.

PEITHO goddess of persuasion and flattery.

PELOPS son of Tantalus. His father served him up as meat in a banquet for the gods[1] (to test their power of knowing everything) and was severely punished for it. The gods restored Pelops to life and even gave him a new shoulder made of ivory, to replace the one that had been eaten. Pelops came to Elis in the Peloponnesus and brought such riches with him that the whole peninsula was named after him ("Island of Pelops"). He was the father of Atreus and Thyestes.

PENTHEUS a legendary king of Thebes whom Dionysus punished for daring to look upon the orgiastic rites of his mother (a Maenad or mystic worshiper of Dionysus), by changing Pentheus into a hare, which was torn to pieces by his mother and her following of women. Cf. Euripides' play *The Bacchae*.

PERSEPHASSA another name for Persephone, the Roman Proserpina. She was the daughter of Zeus and Demeter and was carried off by Hades to be his wife and become queen of the Underworld.

PERSEUS the son of Zeus and Danaë (whom Zeus impregnated in a shower of gold). Perseus slew Medusa, the Gorgon, turning away his eyes. He also killed the sea monster which was threatening Andromeda, and married her.

PHERES father of Admetus (king of Pherae, in Thes-

---

[1] Not to be confused with a later banquet whereat Atreus served up Thyestes' children to him.

saly), who persuaded the Fates to let him off death if someone else died for him. His wife, Alcestis, sacrificed her life for him, but Apollo (a family friend) went down to Hades and brought her back. Cf. Euripides' famous play.

PHINEUS a seer, who blinded his own sons because of an alleged treachery. The gods punished him in turn with blindness and, to torment him, sent the Harpies, who carried away his meals.

PHLEGRAEAN the fields or volcanic plain in the district of Campania (in Italy), where Heracles fought the giants.

PHOCIS a region in central Greece on the gulf of Corinth.

PHOEBE another name for Artemis, sister of Apollo (Phoebus).

PHOEBUS "bright one"—epithet of the god Apollo.

PLEISTHENES father of Tantalus.

PLEISTUS the mythical father of the Corycian Nymphs. Also a river flowing through the vale of Delphi.

POSEIDON the Roman Neptune: god of the sea and of horses, who drove his chariot over the seas and lived in their depths. He was the brother of Zeus and Hades. Also, he invented the bit and the bridle. One of the Athenians' favorite gods.

PRIAM the last king of Troy. His wife was Hecuba, and among his fifty sons and twelve daughters were Hector, Paris, and Cassandra.

PYTHIA also called the Pythoness, high priestess of Apollo at Delphi. After inhaling the intoxicating vapors which rose from the ground in the center of the temple, she uttered the revelations of the god.

SARONIC the Saronic gulf, a stretch of water between the Arachnian Hill and Mount Aegyplanctus.

SCAMANDER a river in Asia Minor near Troy.

SCYLLA a sea monster who sat on the rocks on the
Italian side of the Straits of Messina waiting for
mariners whom she could devour or wreck. Opposite her was the equally dangerous sea monster
Charybdis, a whirlpool ("between Scylla and
Charybdis" = "between the devil and the deep
blue sea").

SCYLLA the daughter of Nisus, king of Megara. He was
besieged in his town by Minos, king of Crete. Scylla
fell in love with Minos and accepted his gifts. She
was willing to cut off from her father's head the
purple lock of hair on which his life depended.
Minos killed him, then turned on Scylla. He drowned
her by tying her by the feet to his departing ship.

SCYTHIA a district beyond northern Greece whose inhabitants were bellicose and savage and made a
special cult of the god Ares. The Scythian bow was
long and flexible, bending either way.

STROPHIUS the Phocian, in whose care Orestes was put
when Aegisthus and Clytemnestra took over the
throne of Argos.

STRYMON a river in Greece, where Orpheus sat dolefully
for seven months after his final loss of Eurydice.

SYRIA a country in Asia Minor along the Mediterranean
coast.

TANTALIDAE the descendants of Tantalus, the worldly,
wealthy king and son of Zeus. After his death he
was punished by Zeus for divulging divine secrets.
He was placed in a lake in Hades and consumed
with eternal hunger and thirst. Each time he stooped
down to drink, the lake receded, and each time he
reached out to pick the branches of fruit which
hung over him he found them just beyond his grasp.
Pelops was his son; Agamemnon and Menelaus
were his great-grandsons.

TARTARUS another name for Hades. Also, a place as far below hell as heaven is above the earth.

THEMIS the goddess of right and law and hospitality, and also the first wife of Zeus. Sometimes said to be the daughter of Uranus and Gaea (Heaven and Earth). During the war with the Titans she descended to earth and taught men justice and moderation. When they became too corrupt she returned to Mount Olympus.

THESEUS the great hero who became the wise and liberal king of Athens. He was the son of Aegeus, husband of Phaedra, and father of Hippolytus by the Amazon queen Hippolyta.

THYESTES a son of Pelops. His brother, Atreus, father of Agamemnon, served up his own children to him at a banquet, in reprisal for his having seduced Atreus's wife. He was the father of Aegisthus.

TITANS the primordial children of Heaven and Earth; giant deities who were overthrown by Zeus and succeeded by the Olympian gods.

TRITON son of Poseidon and Amphitrite, a sea-god who acted as Poseidon's herald. He carried a trident and a conch shell on which he blew fiercely when the seas were to be rough, and sweetly when the seas were to be calm.

TROY also called Ilium, a proud and splendid city in northwestern Asia Minor overlooking the shores of the Thracian Sea.

TYNDAREUS king of Sparta, husband of Leda, and father of Clytemnestra. Also, foster father of Helen.

ZEPHYR the gentle West Wind, who was lightly clad and carried flowers in his scarf.

ZEUS the Roman Jupiter, greatest and most powerful of the Olympian gods.

ACKNOWLEDGMENTS

With Special Gratitude

to Mother Adele M. Fiske, Professor of Classics at Manhattanville College of the Sacred Heart, for use of her illuminating monograph on Aeschylus compared with Eugene O'Neill.

to the old translators of the *Oresteia* and many of the new, whom I have kept at my elbow throughout to check and steady me. Among those who have gone before I feel grateful to Anna Swanwick, E. H. Plumtre, H. Weir-Smythe. . . . Oh, yes—these great scholars may disappoint our ears with their overloaded sentences, their pseudo-Swinburnian, and their desperate effort to be faithful to Greek syntax, but at least in essence they were right in their realization that Greek poetry, even dramatic poetry, was melodious and full of verbal beauty.

Among some of the modern translators I owe a debt to Miss Edith Hamilton—the pioneer in the new approach—to Professor Gilbert Norwood for his perennially useful work on Greek tragedy; to Dr. Peter Arnott for his immensely helpful new *Introduction to the Greek Theatre;* and to Professor Lattimore for his brilliantly concise but searching Introduction to his translation of the *Oresteia,* which outlines almost everything that can be said. I was also excitingly impressed by the fine renderings of Mr. Louis MacNeice and Sir John Sheppard, the one-time Provost of King's College, Cambridge.

If it may not seem presumptuous to call out great names, I should like to put on record the immense help

I have derived from the scholarly pages of Sir Arnold Toynbee, Sir Maurice Bowra, and Sir Arthur Pickard-Cambridge.

In writing my Introduction I was greatly inspired by an essay on Greek Tragedy by Professor Robert Brustein, published in *The Griffin*, November 1959.

With Simple Thanks

to my beloved Clarissa, δόμων ἄγαλμα ("jewel of my house"), for her untarnished faith in my ability to translate Greek drama, for her patient listening to pages of Greek and pages of English, and for her never-ending typing.

to Mr. Robert Bassil of Saginaw (who edits a magazine called *Michigan's Voices*), for some perceptive remarks he made on my first reading to him the draft of *The Agamemnon*.

to Mr. Axel Fabre for being imaginative enough to waive all temporal and temporary requirements and let me live and work in his paradise for Nobel Prize winners at Playa Mimosa, Acapulco.

to the Baroness Françoise d'Aulnis de Bourouille and Mr. Eddie Sleeswicjk for making valuable human suggestions to me after I had read them my Introduction.

to Mrs. Bennet Kassler for putting at my disposal for several weeks a garden in a "landscape by Poussin" at the Chorillo in Taxco, where the grand emotions of Aeschylus were able to pour into my soul unimpeded.

to Mrs. Dorothy MacDonald for her unfailing enthusiasm and generosity, and for making it possible for me to get away from those delights of my eyes—Pandora, Marc-Paul, and Vanessa-Ariadne-Jane (my children)—by lending me her beautiful house and garden to work in, where I completed this whole enterprise.

The text I have used throughout, except for a few instances, is that of the Loeb Classical Library.

MENTOR Classics

☐ **BULFINCH'S MYTHOLOGY, Volume I: The Age of Fable.** A retelling of the myths of ancient Greece and Rome, with Introduction by Palmer Bovie. (#MW1482—$1.50)

☐ **BULFINCH'S MYTHOLOGY, Volumes II and III: The Age of Chivalry and Legends of Charlemagne.** The great legends of the Middle Ages with an Introduction by Palmer Bovie. (#ME1458—$1.75)

☐ **MYTHOLOGY by Edith Hamilton.** A brilliant re-telling of the classic Greek, Roman, and Norse legends of love and adventure. (#MJ1697—$1.95)

☐ **THE ANCIENT MYTHS by Norma Lorre Goodrich.** A vivid re-telling of the great myths of Greece, Egypt, India, Persia, Crete, Sumer, and Rome. (#MY1407—$1.25)

☐ **MYTHS OF THE GREEKS AND ROMANS by Michael Grant.** The world's great myths and their impact on creative arts through the ages. Illustrated.
(#ME1634—$2.50)

☐ **THE METAMORPHOSES by Ovid, translated by Horace Gregory.** Ovid's magnificent collection of legends and myths, translated into vital modern poetry.
(#MJ1551—$1.95)

☐ **THE GREEK EXPERIENCE by C. M. Bowra.** An extraordinary study of Greek culture, its achievements and philosophy. With 48 pages of photos. (#ME1718—$1.75)

Plays in MENTOR Editions

☐ **THE GENIUS OF THE EARLY ENGLISH THEATER edited by Barnet, Berman, and Burto.** Complete plays including three anonymous plays—**Abraham and Isaac, The Second Shepherd's Play,** and **Everyman,** and Marlowe's **Doctor Faustus,** Shakespeare's **Macbeth,** Jonson's **Volpone,** and Milton's **Samson Agonistes.** Also includes critical essays. (#ME1642—$2.25)

☐ **EIGHT GREAT COMEDIES edited by Barnet, Berman, and Burto.** Complete English texts of **The Clouds,** Machiavelli's **Mandragola, Twelfth Night, The Miser, The Beggar's Opera, Importance of Being Earnest, Uncle Vanya, Arms and the Man.** With essays on the comic view. (#ME1340—$1.75)

☐ **EIGHT GREAT TRAGEDIES edited by Barnet, Berman and Burto.** Complete English texts of **Prometheus Bound, Oedipus the King, Hippolytus, King Lear, Ghosts, Miss Julie, On Baile's Strand,** and **Desire Under the Elms.** With essays on the tragic view. (#MJ1510—$1.95)

☐ **THE CLOUDS by Aristophanes, translated and with an Introduction by William Arrowsmith.** Filled with parody, exaggeration, outrageous burlesque, masterfully juggling ideas and reputations, it triumphantly remains as a magnificent display of comic genius. (#MW1678—$1.50)

☐ **THE BIRDS by Aristophanes, translated and with an Introduction by William Arrowsmith.** A modern translation of one of the greatest comedies ever written. Includes a glossary and a complete set of explanatory notes. (#MW1671—$1.50)

☐ **THE MENTOR BOOK OF SHORT PLAYS edited by Richard H. Goldstone and Abraham H. Lass.** A treasury of drama by some of the finest playwrights of the century including Thornton Wilder, Tennessee Williams, Gore Vidal, and many others. (#ME1504—$1.75)

The MENTOR Philosophers

A distinguished series of volumes presenting in historical order the basic writings of the outstanding philosophers of the Western world—from the Middle Ages to the present time.

☐ **THE AGE OF BELIEF: THE MEDIEVAL PHILOSOPHERS** edited by Anne Fremantle. Basic writings of St. Augustine, Boethius, Abelard, St. Bernard, St. Thomas Aquinas, Duns Scotus, William of Ockham and others. (#MW1258—$1.50)

☐ **THE AGE OF REASON: The 17TH CENTURY PHILOSOPHERS** edited by Stuart Hampshire. Bacon, Pascal, Hobbes, Galileo, Descartes, Spinoza, Leibniz. (#MW1428—$1.50)

☐ **THE AGE OF ENLIGHTENMENT: THE 18TH CENTURY PHILOSOPHERS** edited by Isaiah Berlin. Locke, Berkeley, Voltaire, Hume, Reid, Condillac, Hamann. (#MY1213—$1.25)

☐ **THE AGE OF IDEOLOGY: THE 19TH CENTURY PHILOSOPHERS** edited by Henry D. Aiken. Kant, Fichte, Hegel, Schopenhauer, Comte, Mill, Spencer, Marx, Nietzsche, Kierkegaard. (#MW1452—$1.50)

☐ **THE AGE OF ANALYSIS: THE 20TH CENTURY PHILOSOPHERS** edited by Morton White. Peirce, Whitehead, James, Dewey, Bertrand Russell, Wittgenstein, Croce, Bergson, Sartre, Santayana, and others. (#MW1179—$1.50)

THE NEW AMERICAN LIBRARY, INC.,
P.O. Box 999, Bergenfield, New Jersey 07621

Please send me the MENTOR BOOKS I have checked above. I am enclosing $_____(please add 50¢ to this order to cover postage and handling). Send check or money order—no cash or C.O.D.'s. Prices and numbers are subject to change without notice.

Name_____

Address_____

City_____State_____Zip Code_____
Allow at least 4 weeks for delivery